Co
For
Murder

DARREN KIRBY

Copyright © 2012 Darren Kirby

All rights reserved.

ISBN: 1470079100
ISBN-13: 9781470079109

Cover Design by Lindsay Breen
www.lindsaybreencovers.com

OTHER WRITINGS BY DARREN KIRBY

~Short Stories~

Pins And Dolls

ACKNOWLEDGMENTS

As is the case with every writer, there are numerous people that I need to thank for their contributions, in small ways and in large, as without them this book would not be in your hands.

First, I want to thank my wonderful wife, Amy, who puts up with my constant "latest ideas" and never flinches. You are the anchor that keeps me from spinning off the planet into oblivion. I love you more than words can say.

To Bob: I miss your perspective on life and writing. You'll never be forgotten. Rest in peace, cowboy.

To the rest of the writer gang: Marla, Donna, April, Gail and Marjorie. I thank you all for pushing, pulling and prodding me with my writing. I'm the better for it, and your counsel will never be forgotten. You ladies rock!

To my beta readers: a huge thank you for all of your feedback, contributions, and generally cleaning up the crap to make this as good as it could be.

For everyone else that helped but that I did not name, your contributions were invaluable as well. You all had a hand in helping me grow as a writer with this novel, and for that I can't thank you enough.

From here, things will only go up. I hope I entertain as many people as possible along the way.

~Darren
Wisconsin, January 2012

"Three may keep a secret, if two of them are dead."

~Poor Richard's Almanac
July, 1735

1

"You know, you could get lost and wind up dead way up there in the sticks," said Carlos.

Sammy threw a glance over to Carlos, who was working his way up the sidewalk on his knees, unrolling the sod. An immigrant from Mexico, he had been working with Sammy for at least three years. Sammy could tell that Carlos was chuckling to himself; he always made himself laugh.

"Only if I were a stupid gringo. Or if I had you as a guide," Sammy retorted.

Carlos just continued working, shaking his head in amusement. Sammy and Carlos had always gotten along well, and this was just the latest in their usual back-and-forth banter. Sammy also liked to use Carlos's Hispanic lingo from time to time, just to rile him up.

"It's amazing *any* work gets done between you two yapping and carrying on like that," Brian piped up from across the parking lot.

Sammy finished cutting out a notch in the sod for the concrete cylinder that would soon hold a light pole, then stood and pointed his sod knife toward Brian. "Yeah, like you do any actual work out here. You know I could beat you sod laying with an arm behind my back, rookie."

Brian finished cutting a small hole for a sprinkler head, then turned and looked at Sammy. He couldn't help but start to laugh. Tony, working just down from Brian, whispered loudly to Brian: "Don't do it, man, don't do it."

"What?" Brian asked Tony loudly. "Don't do it? Man, he's not that good."

Tony looked up from his work, a small grin on his face. He knew just what to say to get him going. "I just don't want to see you goin' home to your girlfriend cryin' and whinin' that you got beat, that's all."

Carlos and Sammy started laughing as Brian got a big smile on his face, hanging his head in mock defeat. Then Brian looked back at Sammy, still smiling. "Need your lackeys to defend you, eh? I bet you wouldn't even be halfway done when I finish."

"How much?" Sammy asked.

"What?"

"How *much*?"

"Dude, you wouldn't win." Brian got up and walked to the pallet with rolls of sod, grabbed one and carried it back to where he'd been working. Sammy watched him work. He was a good kid; cocky, but a good kid. He'd be a senior in high school this fall, playing wide receiver on the varsity football team. He had a girlfriend, but that didn't stop other girls from trying, and who could blame them – he had the good looks that Sammy had always wanted. Not that Sammy wasn't good looking, but his genetics just didn't provide him with the Roman god-like looks that some others had. His olive complexion was even darker working out in sun like he did (mahogany, he liked to tell women), and he was fit and toned. But his face wasn't anything to write home about, and the fact that his mother couldn't afford braces for his teeth meant that his smile was perpetually crooked. Cute to some women, however.

"Are you done fooling around? What's the bet?" Sammy asked again.

"I don't want to take your money; it wouldn't be fair."

Carlos and Tony looked at Brian, then to Sammy. They could read Sammy's face, and they knew what was coming. What they didn't yet know was just how close Brian would come.

Sammy walked over to the pallet with the sod rolls, and pulled a wad of bills from his front pocket. He proceeded to lay out three twenty dollar bills. As if by magic, Troy and Kelly, who were working on a retaining wall along the back side of the property, materialized and hovered by the sod, eager looks on their faces. "Sixty says you can't do it."

All eyes turned to the rookie. He kept working, pretending that he wasn't the subject of the statement. He let the silence continue.

"Fine, a Benji then." Sammy added two more bills.

"Whoa, dude!" exclaimed Kelly. "If you don't do it, I will just for a shot at that pot."

Brian finished up his sod roll and walked nonchalantly over to the group. He stood facing Sammy, watching, evaluating. Finally, he reached into his back pocket for his wallet, excavating bills to double the pot. Kelly ran off to grab Hugh, who was running the four-wheeler prepping another area for sod the next day. Carlos swept up the cash and folded it into the breast pocket on his dingy t-shirt for safekeeping.

"So where are we gonna do this?" asked Brian, looking from Sammy to Carlos.

Carlos pointed to two small islands in the parking lot that still needed to have sod fit into them. "Use those."

"You're really only going to use one arm against me?" Brian asked Sammy.

"Yup."

Kelly and Hugh returned and sat down on a nearby sidewalk, grateful for the break. Carlos positioned himself between the islands and his co-workers and laid out the simple rules: whoever finished laying the sod completely on their island first would be the winner. Sammy could only use one arm for the competition, and he chose his right arm. With a quick countdown, they were off.

Everyone got into the competition, shouting encouragement as well as insults. Sammy got to his island with the sod and rolled it down his arm with a quick motion, holding onto the end with his hand. The sod ended perfectly in the corner, and he easily maneuvered it into position then took off for the pallet for his next roll.

Brian also easily placed his first roll, keeping pace with Sammy. They each returned with their second rolls and flung them out into position. Sammy chose to put his in a place where cutting wasn't necessary, but Brian landed his on a sprinkler head and had to cut that out to fit. In that short time, Sammy managed to pick his third roll and return, flinging it out into another corner, though this would need trimming.

Ignoring the necessary cutting for the time being, Sammy again raced back to the pallet, as did Brian, who was now one full roll behind their crew leader. Brian stuck to his plan, cutting this third roll to accommodate the concrete light pole base. Sammy again chose to roll out this fourth roll and ignore the needed trimming.

Allowing himself a quick glance, Brian began to sweat even more looking at Sammy's progress. He was losing to a guy using just one arm! His girlfriend was going to kill him – that money was going to pay for a really nice dinner that they were taking her parents to that weekend.

Sammy returned with his fifth and final sod roll, sweat pouring off of him. He dropped the sod on the only patch of dirt left, then drew his sod knife and began to work on cutting out the corner for the concrete light pole base on his island. Brian finish up his cuts and ran to get his fourth roll of sod.

Along the far sidewalk, a small crowd had gathered, curious about the shouting and activity. Sammy had made cuts for the two sprinkler heads, trimmed excess away from the concrete edges where sod was hanging off, and was at his last roll. Brian had quickly placed his fourth roll, pleased that he could lay it clean and grab his last roll. He might be able to win yet.

Sammy quickly unrolled part of the sod and yanked one end into position. With the experience of thousands of sod cuts, he instantly judged where to make his last incision. Brian had returned to his island and proceeded to place his last piece. He knew he could do it, just one more cut to go.

"Done!" shouted Sammy.

Brian finished his cut, fit the edge into the sod puzzle and jumped clear of his island. Everyone came over to inspect their work, to make sure that neither of them cut any corners or placed their rolls in a sloppy manner.

Kelly shook his head in amazement. "Sammy wins *again!*"

Brian sauntered over to Sammy's island, knowing that he'd been beaten, but wanting to see his work just the same.

"Shit," Sammy said, "I thought this would be the time that I lost, bro! Nice job."

Brian got a sly grin on his face, not fully believing that he could have lost to someone using only one arm. Those sod rolls weren't too light, either. He couldn't take his eyes off of the newly laid grass. "I-I just can't believe that I couldn't take you. I mean, you were only using one arm. What the hell?"

Carlos walked over and bestowed the two hundred dollars to Sammy. "Winner, and still champion!"

Sammy flipped through the bills, then separated out his five bills and shoved them in his pocket. He grabbed Brian's hand and slapped the remaining money into his palm. "I know you were going to use that to take your girlfriend and her parents out to dinner this weekend. You drove me hard, man. You deserve it." Brian looked down at his hand in disbelief.

He slapped Brian on the shoulder and offered a crooked smile. Everyone went back to their work, and Sammy headed to his truck. If he wasn't careful, one of these times he would actually lose the bet.

Back at his truck, he grabbed the clipboard off of the passenger seat and started flipping through the landscape layout designs. If the weather held, they might actually be able to finish up this job tomorrow, which would put them a full day ahead of schedule, and a good chunk of change of additional profit into the company with labor savings.

Sammy pulled his smart phone out of the cup holder and called up the local TV station website. On their radar feed, he could see that showers were heading their way, and would probably be there in time to ruin much of tomorrow's progress.

"Shit, not what I needed," he grumbled. Looking out at his crew he yelled: "Carlos! We got problems."

2

"What's happening, amigo?"

"Jump in, I got a few things for you."

Carlos climbed into the passenger side of Sammy's work truck. Sammy passed him his smart phone with the radar feed still showing.

"Looks like you'll be dancing through the drops tomorrow." Sammy pointed to the radar view on the phone. "I was hoping that we could finish this job tomorrow, but this weather may say otherwise."

Carlos handed the smart phone back, nodding. Sammy then gave him the clipboard and started pointing at the layout design for the current project they were working on. "Hugh is working on this large swath in the northeast corner, and he should have that ready for the hydroseeding tomorrow. Based on how the weather looks, you'll have to make the call early if it should still be done or not. The guys that own this property have a dozen other properties in the metro area, and I want things done right, not fast. We can hit that next week if need be.

"From what I saw earlier today, Kelly and Troy should only need to put finishing touches on the retaining wall tomorrow.

It looks great; they always do a nice job. And you and the rest of the gang can finish up the sod work around the parking lot and sidewalks. Clean up will be priority, same reason as the hydroseeding call.

"I'll be available by cell until probably the early afternoon. Darn engineers haven't yet figured out how to make a cell tower that grows like a tree."

They both sat in silence for a few minutes as Carlos looked over the plans on the clipboard and anticipated possible scenarios for tomorrow. Satisfied, he put the clipboard up on the dash, then turned toward Sammy.

"You got a few minutes, amigo?" asked Carlos.

"Sure, what's up?"

"My boy the other day, he mentioned geocaching. Said a friend of his from school went with his father and couldn't stop jabbering about it. Now he wants to go, but, I...I don't know what it's about. I know you go, quite a bit. Is it hard? What do you need to do it?"

Sammy's face beamed, both at being asked for his expertise and for getting to talk about geocaching. He was hoping that sometime soon he would be able to take a month-long trip to Europe or Asia to do geocaching. It was such a unique sport that virtually anyone could get involved with.

"First off, Carlos, you will have a great time with your son. I can guarantee that. Getting started with geocaching is very easy. It's basically like a high-tech treasure hunt. The only piece of equipment that you need is a handheld GPS unit, and you may already have one. Or your cell phone probably has a GPS app for it."

Carlos nodded his understanding.

"You'll then need to find out where some caches are that you can find. There are a number of websites that exist just to help people find new caches and for people to post their own cache locations."

Sammy could see that this last part was confusing to Carlos; he always got a real serious look when he was trying to figure something out.

"Wait, that doesn't make sense to me. What's the fun if people, they are just giving you the location? What's the point?" Carlos asked, shrugging.

Sammy laughed. That was the usual first question that he was always asked by someone just learning what everything was about. He explained that they were only providing the coordinates, and that the cache itself was still hidden and needed to be found. Part of the fun was also in seeing who else had found the cache, and what goodies were inside.

"But Joseph, he told me that his friend and his father had found a cache that was a lookout tower. How does that work?" asked Carlos.

"Oh sure, there are a lot of those. They'll sometimes be referred to as an earthcache or a virtual cache. Usually they have some geological feature or other Earth science education. I like doing those from time to time, and you can take pictures of yourself at the location. That would be a great idea for you and Joseph."

Sammy got out one of his GPS units that he had with him. He showed Carlos how to operate the unit, where to put in the coordinates, waypoints and a few other useful features. On his smart phone, he showed Carlos a few of the geocaching websites and where the coordinates could be found, who else had found them, and the status of the cache from the last finder.

For Sammy, one of the challenges to the sport of geocaching was being the first to find a geocache and log it. "There's just something special in being the very first person to go through the hoops and roadblocks with finding a cache," he explained.

"Thank you, my friend," said Carlos. "But, I am still a little afraid of trying this. You know that I don't talk so good to start with, and when I get upset I go back to my Spanish. I don't want to be swearing up a storm in front of my kid."

Sammy thought for a moment, then offered a suggestion. If Carlos would tell him where he and his son wanted to go, Sammy would loan him one of his GPS units preloaded with a few easy to find geocaches. That way they could have the fun of finding them without worrying about the technology part for now.

Carlos got a wide smile and nodded enthusiastically. "Yes, that would be excellent! Thank you, Sam, thank you!"

"No problem, Carlos," Sammy replied, chuckling. "Just remember to give me a few days lead time before you leave so I can get you all set up, okay?"

"Yes, okay, definitely. I will do that."

Carlos grabbed Sammy's hand and shook it vigorously in appreciation. He exited the truck and walked around the front to the driver's side. He put his hand on the pillar just behind the door and leaned in toward Sammy. "What you want me to do if Ronald tries anything?"

Sammy scrunched up his face in disgust. Ever since Sammy got promoted to crew leader, Ronald, a fellow crew leader, had tried to sabotage his work and that of his crew. Every time he had been able to show that his crew's work was top-notch. But he wouldn't put it past Ronald to stoop to trying to wreck their work just as he left on a day off and would be too far away to return in a timely manner.

"You got a camera with you? One that shows the date?"

Carlos nodded.

"Take a few shots before it gets too dark tonight. Key pieces are the wall, sod work, hydroseed prep, and so forth. We'll need to document our progress in case he gets stupid. Tomorrow, if anything is touched, take pictures again to show what happened."

"Ah, good plan! Okay, you don't get lost, now. I don't want to come find you!"

Sammy half-grinned and Carlos slugged his shoulder and smiled, then took off to go back to rolling out sod.

* * *

Leaving the work site, Sammy radioed headquarters. He let them know that he was heading back in, and that his crew would be working a couple more hours before coming in themselves. He made good time back to base, having beat the start of rush hour traffic. Truck parked, paperwork given to the office manager, Sammy jogged out to his Jeep and took off in a cloud of dust and smoke.

Five minutes later, he pulled into the parking lot of his favorite outdoor store. Sammy loved to try out new gear, and he'd recently started trying to court gear manufacturers to have him do reviews on their new products, posting them on his blog site. So far, he hadn't had any takers, but with the thousands of hits his blog got every week, he knew that it would only be a matter of time.

Inside, he quickly found the new hiking socks that he'd been wanting to try out. It would make a great blog post next week on his gear review section. He briefly scanned through the GPS receiver units, checking to see if any new models had arrived yet. His last stop was the camping and hiking section. He had just upgraded his backpack to one that had a slightly large capacity, but yet weighed a little less – win/win in his world. He paid for the spendy new socks - $8 a pair – then headed out again.

On his way home Sammy made a short stop at the grocery store for a few last-minute items for the trip. Then he headed home. And Ronald better not strike while he was away, or Sammy would have his head.

3

"Finally, home sweet home." said Sammy to himself.
Silence returned his greeting.
Closing the door, he carried his bag of goodies through the tidy living room into the stark white kitchen. No papers hung on the fridge door with magnets, no towels folded neatly over the handle on the oven door, nothing out of place on the white flecked Formica counter. Functional was what he called it, blah is what his mother called it. He didn't often cook, for himself or others, and rarely spent much time there. Why should he make it pretty when no one would be there to appreciate it?

With a quick turn of his wrists, he turned the bag upside down on the small counter and the contents formed a small, unstable pyramid of boxes and cans. Sammy folded up the paper bag and slid it under the sink, then cleared off the counter of his purchases. He broke off a banana from the bunch and peeled it as he made his way through the living room into the bedroom.

Sammy plopped down into the hard wooden chair in front of his desk and took a big bite out of the fresh peeled banana. He lifted the screen on the laptop that was situated in the middle of the worn desk. The screen popped to life almost instantly – he hated waiting for it to boot up, and left it in sleep mode versus turning it off. He started his web browser, then picked his usual geocache website from his favorites list.

He first checked the status of the caches that he had placed in a few choice areas. All of them appeared to still be in good shape, at least according to the last reports of the cachers who had recently found them. Then he did a search of caches for the area where he was going to be camping at with his friend, John, over the weekend. As the search results came back and the icons flashed up on the screen, Sammy saw something he hadn't anticipated.

"Are you shitting me?"

Amidst all of the different colored icons on the screen, one stood out. That was because when he looked at this results screen just this morning, there were only ten caches in total. Now there were eleven. And the eleventh one was out a ways from the rest of the others, secluded. And better still, no one had yet found it. Cachers, hard-core ones anyway, always liked to be the first ever to locate a cache. This was his golden opportunity.

Nearly falling out of his chair, Sammy ripped his cell phone out of his jeans pocket. Typing furiously on the tiny keyboard, he sent off a quick text to his friend John.

New cache to find. Just posted. We'll be FTF!

The seconds ticked by like hours as Sammy waited for a reply.

Sweet! Time leaving?

That was a good question, when should they leave - tomorrow morning? Knowing that they would want to head out to find at least one cache tomorrow, he figured that they should be on the road no later than eight tomorrow. Sammy quickly tapped out the response and sent it off. John's reply came back a minute later.

K. I'll be ready

Sammy snorted a chuckle. John would be ready to go by eight? Yeah, that would be the day. If there was one thing Sammy could count on, it would be that John wouldn't be ready to go when he showed up in the morning.

He returned to the search results on the screen, and noticed something that he hadn't seen the first time. The new cache wasn't just a single, but was the start of a multi-cache. Finding this first one would provide coordinates that would lead to a second with more coordinates to a third, and so on. Suddenly, Sammy wasn't just excited to be a First To Find on this new cache, but a First To Find for this new multi-cache. He was nearly shaking with anticipation.

John would be ready to go by eight tomorrow morning; Sammy would make damn sure of that.

4

"Don't work too much longer, Johnny. Ain't you got an adventure to get to or something?"

He hated being called 'Johnny'. Every time someone called him that he would grit his teeth and cringe on the inside. Some days it annoyed him so much that he thought his teeth would explode from the pressure he put on them.

"No way, Tommy. I'm just about ready to get the heck out of Dodge."

It wasn't really a jab back at Tom, but it made John feel like he won a little victory by calling him 'Tommy'. At least he felt like he was defending himself, even if it was only in his own mind.

"You keep putting in overtime like you have, and you'll be taking Sharon's job." Sharon was their mutual supervisor at Bradly & Associates Accounting. She was rumored to be on the short list for an upcoming promotion, which meant handling some of the larger accounts. "You know that's got my name written all over it." Tom chuckled.

"Don't worry, I won't forget about all of your hard work when I move into that corner office," replied John. *Because there isn't any to forget*, he added silently.

Tom slung his laptop bag over his shoulder and headed towards the elevators, his head shaking. John watched him go and prayed that Tom would never become his boss. He'd probably quit if that happened.

As the elevator doors closed, John's cell phone beeped at him from his desk. He picked it up and saw that his friend Sammy had sent him a text message.

New cache to find. Just posted. We'll be FTF!

First to find – their holy grail at the moment. He and Sammy had been geocaching for a few years together, but had never been able to be the first to find any of the caches. Once, they had been close, having found a cache online that no one had posted to yet. But when they found the cache, the log book had already been signed, and not more than 30 minutes prior to them finding it. Now, they had another chance to be the first to find a cache, and this one had a better than average chance at working out in their favor: where they were going, not many people went, and even fewer did geocaching.

Sweet! Time leaving? John texted back to his friend.

He was waiting for some snide comment from him. John was never one to be ready to go at a certain time, except for work. He just had some fundamental flaw in his character that would preclude him from being on time for things. But when it came to being on time for work, he was always there, never late. John chalked it up to God having a sense of humor at his expense.

8am. And if u r not ready, I'm leaving w/out u. LOL

John doubted that he'd leave without him, but you never could tell with Sammy. Sometimes he would just decide on something and then do it. He didn't do it with malice either, just that something clicked in his head and he would go off in a new direction. It got John mad sometimes, as he much preferred to be methodical with things. That's probably why he enjoyed his work so much; accountants needed to be methodical when going through a company's books.

K. I'll be ready. John replied. He could imagine Sammy chuckling at his response. But maybe he would surprise him this time...

Turning his attention back to his computer, John saved his spreadsheet , set his Outlook to autoreply that he was out, then logged off. He put his office phone to his Out of Town message, then jotted down a quick note to leave for his boss. Sharon was great to work for, except she liked to "forget" about people taking vacations. John couldn't remember the last time she took one.

He stuck the Post-It to her desk phone, then hopped in the elevator and rode it to the second floor. Downtown Minneapolis had a number of positives about it, not the least of which was the SkyWay system that allowed one to walk from building to building at the second story level. Crossing over the SkyWay to the adjacent parking garage, he caught a beautiful view of the late afternoon sun. Then it hit him: he had the perfect plan in case he wasn't ready in time tomorrow morning. Sammy wouldn't leave without him once he showed him the new toy he would pick up on the way home.

He entered the parking garage from the SkyWay, locating his Jeep in his usual spot one slot down from the corner where drivers had a tendency to clip cars in the end slot as they went past. He fired it up and took off for his favorite sporting goods store.

Getting out of downtown was the usual headache that he had to endure on a daily basis: honking from pissed off drivers, people yelling through the windows of their cars and communicating in other colorful ways. If he didn't enjoy his job so much he would have found a different one in one of the suburbs. People could be complete nutjobs out on the road.

At the sporting goods store, John quickly found his way to the hiking and camping section. He moved past the various GPS units and settled his eyes on the new toy: a pair of walkie-talkies. But these weren't just your average child walkie-talkies, they had a 3-mile range, GPS locator beacon, and could take a headset for hands-free operation. He picked out matching jawbone headsets and grabbed a couple of packages of rechargeable batteries at the register.

    Ready or not, Sammy would be too excited to leave without him. He was a sucker for anything new.

5

Multi-cache. Sammy could barely contain his excitement over their luck. He added the newest cache to the list of caches to download to his GPS – fifteen of them in all. Not that they would get to all of them, but he always liked to be prepared in case things went really well. He pulled his newest, and therefore his favorite, GPS unit from a small drawer in the old desk, along with a USB cable. He plugged one end of the cable into the GPS unit and the other end into his laptop. After a few seconds, the laptop recognized the GPS unit, and he proceeded to download the coordinates for all of the geocaches.

Sammy headed down to the garage for his townhouse, where he also stored his camping gear. Organization was key for him, as he accumulated so much gear, both from his own purchases as well as the occasional product review that he did. He liked to keep the gear and provide long-term usage updates on them periodically. Some of the manufacturers didn't always appreciate this aspect of his reviewing process, but he wanted to report on products as real users would use them, not from a use-once-and-toss-it mentality.

Packing for Sammy was easy, because he had a base set of gear that he always brought with him. To that, he added other items to round out his full gear set. What he brought depended a lot on the weather and time of year, plus who he was going with. Since John had plenty of his own stuff, Sammy could travel lighter than he usually did when he went with others who didn't have all of the equipment or knowledge that Sammy did. This trip would also be in nice summer weather, which necessitated that he have lighter-weight as well as light-colored clothes. He'd pack those last.

Stretching his arm to the back of one of the shelves, he reached behind a box filled with some of his heavy winter clothing. His fingers closed around the cold plastic handle. Carefully he pulled out a small square black metal case that looked like a miniature brief case. He carried it around the passenger side of his Jeep and laid the case on the hood. He pressed his right thumb to a built-in fingerprint scanner on the edge of the case, and a few seconds later the closure pins popped open. Sammy's new toy rested comfortably in its gray foam slot.

He picked up the 9mm matte black handgun, admiring it. He was happy with the recent purchase, but so far hadn't told anyone else about it. His mother felt that guns were unnecessary, even though she lived in Chicago and worked downtown, sometimes into the evening. His friend John wasn't much better. Sammy had casually brought up the subject one time a while ago, but John looked at guns with a hefty amount of skepticism. To his way of thinking, only people who couldn't use their mind would resort to using such things. Sammy was more pragmatic, more open to the way things really were. In a couple of weeks he would start going to classes to learn how to use it, in case he ever needed to.

He didn't think that he would need it this weekend, but while he was adventurous, he certainly wasn't foolhardy, contrary to what John thought. He took out the two loaded magazines for the gun, and put them and the gun in the glove box of his Jeep. You never knew when you might meet some crazy son of a bitch out there.

Sammy closed the case and returned it to its hiding spot. He headed back into the townhouse to pack his clothes, put together some food, and make sure his GPS was fully loaded with the coordinates.

* * *

Stepping through the door that led from the kitchen to the garage, John pressed the white button on the wall. With a few squeaks of protest, the garage door lifted and sunlight filled the small interior. John sipped coffee from his favorite travel mug as he shuffled to the far rear corner of the garage where he stored his camping gear. Even though it was a vacation day and he should have been excited to go camping and geocaching with his friend, John found it difficult to roll out of bed at seven-thirty that morning. After a quick stop at the bathroom, he had made coffee to help jump-start his day, but the caffeine hadn't hit him yet. And now he was down to twenty minutes before Sammy said he would arrive.

Still half-asleep, John jammed his toes on the cold, heavy steel of a vehicle jack. Doubling over, he nearly dropped his coffee mug, which would have made a painful situation even worse. Mumbling under his breath, he stagger-shuffled the remaining few feet to the wooden shelves. Wide awake from the subsiding pain, he proceeded to pull a variety of items off the shelf and toss them into the open back of his Jeep: his tent, sleeping bag, backpack and hiking pack. He would have to put it all together once they got where they were going as he didn't have time now to pack it all up in the backpack.

Grabbing his coffee mug from the shelf, he drained it hoping for a faster hit of the caffeine, then headed back into the house for a refill and to get his clothes. Fortunately, he had packed his clothes and food while he chatted with his girlfriend the night before. Heading back out to the garage, he added them to the accumulated gear in the back of the Jeep. Just as he was about to head back in for his coffee, Sammy honked his horn as he pulled into the driveway, Eminem blasting from the stereo.

"Damn, I figured I'd have to bang on the door to get you up!"

"You nearly did. Come in, I got us a new toy."

Sammy followed John into the kitchen. He grinned as he saw the half-empty pot of coffee on the counter. "You office dwellers might as well have an intravenous line in your arm feeding you coffee. I'd sleep through your job if I had to do it."

John didn't take the bait, instead tossing a plastic bag at Sammy. He caught it, then pulled out a new walkie-talkie set and two headsets that John had purchased the night before.

"Whoa! We've been talking about getting these for a while. When'd you get 'em?"

"Last night," said John as he went into his bedroom. "Let me change quick, get a java refill, and we can head out."

Sammy took a steak knife from the utensil drawer and cut open the plastic packaging on the walkie-talkies. He added the fully charged batteries to each one, then plugged in one of the headsets. As he clipped the walkie-talkie to his waist and put on the headset, John emerged from his bedroom.

"From what I've read," said John, "we should be able to use these at highway speeds. The headsets have some special circuitry that helps to isolate the human voice and discard other sounds. Pick the one you like?"

"I'm all set. What do I owe you?"

"Nada. This is payback for the Twins-Yankees game last month."

"Hey, you're alright, no matter what your mother says about you."

Sammy had a wide grin on his face as John shot him a look. He quickly refilled his travel mug then ushered Sammy out into the garage and locked the door.

"You've got all of your stuff packed?" asked Sammy.

"All that matters is that it's all in the Jeep, and I'm ready to go by eight in the morning. I should get a freaking award or something."

Sammy laughed and hopped into his Jeep. He fired it up and took off, with John close behind. It was a great start to a beautiful day.

6

"Aw, shit. Seriously?" asked Sammy.

He had seen the black cloud just as they pulled out of John's neighborhood and got onto the interstate. It stood out because everywhere else looked bright and sunny, except for this black-as-ink cloud. And now it was hovering over them, stalking them as they went down the interstate. That's when the first big drop hit his windshield.

"Seriously what?" asked John in his ear. They had the new walkie-talkies on and the headsets were set to voice-activation.

"Seriously rain," replied Sammy.

More big drops started to hit the windshield. And his head. And the passenger seat. Then everywhere.

"Should have put on the soft covers. Dang, those are some huge raindrops!" said John.

As they slowed to merge from I-694 onto I-94, the cloud tore open and dumped on them. So much for the beautiful, sunny day. John could hear Sammy's headset pick up a few choice words as they accelerated East on the interstate. And then, as quickly as it hit, the black cloud disappeared and bright sunlight engulfed them once more.

"Wow, that was weird. You ever had that happen to you?" asked John.

"My Mom said stuff like that was supposed to be a warning or something. Like something bad was going to happen. Bunch of crap if you ask me."

"Another old wives tale. But just to be safe, you didn't walk under my ladder before we left, did you?"

Sammy chuckled. "Sure did. That's not bad, is it?"

* * *

The rest of the nearly five-hour trip through Minnesota and Wisconsin was uneventful. The sky remained clear, which helped to dry everything that had gotten wet in the brief downpour. As they drove north off of I-94, first on highway 53, then on highway 63, the size of the cities and towns dropped, and the amount of forest rose. Neither of them had been this far north in Wisconsin before, and they were both in awe of the density and beauty of the woods. It seemed to go on forever.

"How can these places stay in business?" asked John over the radio. They had just passed a small, local bar and restaurant, and that was about the only building that they had seen that wasn't blown over or falling apart from age. Hayward seemed to be fairly good sized, even sporting a Walgreen's drug store, but it quickly vanished in favor of near-nothingness.

"I don't know. They must rely on the tourists. But I don't see many of those."

John glanced down at his gas gauge. It showed that he was nearly empty.

"We should have stopped for gas back there. I'm about on fumes."

"Not to worry, my friend. There's a hole-in-the-wall town up the road that we can stop at for gas."

The early afternoon sun beat down on them as they pulled into the tiny town of Drummond. A faded and crooked town sign listed the population at 541 people. As they pulled into the only gas station in town, a lone rusty pickup pulled away and headed further north.

"Boy, when you said hole-in-the-wall, you weren't kidding," said John.

He hopped out and went to the pump, searching around for a credit card reader, a touch screen, anything to indicate how to start the pump.

"Hey!" Sammy shouted from the door of the tiny building. "It's pre-internet. Lift the nozzle and swing the metal plate over the hole where the nozzle sat. That will reset the dials and you can start pumping. Come in once you've filled both Jeeps."

"Amazing," mumbled John to no one. "This from the guy who practically worships technology."

He finished gassing up the Jeeps, then headed in to pay. The whole time, he only saw one other car pass by on the highway. Inside, it was jammed with every conceivable convenience store item imaginable. And at the counter, Sammy was leaning in chatting with the cute brunette employee. She couldn't have been more than twenty, and it didn't hurt that she had the measurements of a swimsuit model.

John grabbed a couple bottles of water from the old drink cooler in the back, then strode up to the counter where Sammy was trying to put his moves on the attractive attendant.

"You really should come out with us. Geocaching is an incredible adventure. And don't worry, I'll keep you safe." Sammy winked at her as a grin spread across his face.

She smiled and looked down, obviously taken with Sammy.

"I'll think about it," she replied with a smile. "This town has nothing, and I'm dying for a little fun."

"Found yourself a new geocache partner?" asked John.

"Oh, sounds like someone's jealous. I'm Jamie." She shook John's hand.

"John," he said, introducing himself. "Sammy and I have a full weekend of geocaching ahead of us, or did he fail to mention that during all of his sweet talk?"

"Hey, just because you're tied down doesn't mean I can't spend time with some interesting people," Sammy retorted.

"Don't worry, guys," said Jamie. "I'm sure you'll have more fun than you can handle out there."

She rang them up for the gas and water, then slipped Sammy a small scrap of paper which he promptly put in his pocket. They grabbed the bottles and headed out.

Firing up the Jeeps again, the friends headed across highway 63 onto Forest Road 213. Immediately they felt like they were transported to a different world. The road was surrounded by trees, and the few lakes they did pass could barely be seen through all of the intense green foliage and brown tree trunks. Along the way, roads would occasionally take off in various directions from the main paved road they were on. Some were dirt driveways for the few people who had vacation homes this far north. Some were used for federal or DNR employees whose work necessitated their presence in this beautiful setting. Still others, which were paved, led around the forest to various camping areas, picnic areas, boat launches, or other places for visitors.

The most significant sign they had seen after nearly 20 minutes of driving was for Twin Lakes campground. John had been talking with his girlfriend about the two of them going camping, and this might be an excellent place; he'd have to remember to mention it to her next week.

"So, how much farther is it, bro?" asked John over the headset.

"We should be nearing the turn-off point. I think it's an old logging road, so we'll have to switch to four-wheel drive."

"Translation: we're not even close."

Sammy laughed in John's ear. "Trust me, it'll be worth it."

"We better be the first to find this sucker, and it better be worth it. That's all I'm saying."

Shortly after passing the campground sign, the road name changed to Forest Road 214, then that split off and they continued on Forest Road 212. A few more minutes, and Sammy slowed down, craning his head to see where the logging road was.

As they rounded a corner near an unnamed lake on their right, the logging road appeared. They shifted into four-high and turned left down the dirt logging path, which was nothing more than two strips of bare dirt with grass in the middle. As they went deeper, the trail got rougher and wetter. Not wanting to get stuck, they shifted into four-low, which allowed them greater torque on the wheels, but meant that they were limited in speed. Not that they felt like bouncing around like ping-pong balls.

After nearly 30 minutes of slow, jostling progress, they entered a large, natural clearing. They pulled off the trail and parked, happy to find that the ground was dry. The open space provided sunlight and the wind was able to make it to the ground, helping to prevent a constant soppiness that other areas seemed to maintain.

John got out of his Jeep and slowly looked around. He was awestruck with the beauty and solitude. Silently he said a prayer of thanks for the safe passage and the privilege to be there.

"Come on, God-boy, we've got things to do and a cache to find," said Sammy. "You can talk with your invisible friends later."

"Don't go dissing God, man. You might regret it."

7

They each started grabbing gear out of their Jeeps and did a short hike to the far edge of the clearing. As they walked there, they noticed a ring of large rocks with ashes in the middle and a few ends of burned branches. Apparently, they weren't the first to have used this area as a campsite.

Sammy pitched his tent quickly and arranged the things he needed inside. John took his time as he simply enjoyed the wonderful day. To help speed things along, Sammy offered to get the remainder of their gear out and setup. He hiked the short distance back to their vehicles, and stopped at the passenger side of his Jeep.

He threw a quick glance over his shoulder at John, who was still engaged with his tent and not paying attention to what Sammy was doing. Turning back, Sammy opened the glove box and slowly took out the handgun and a loaded magazine. Gently he placed the magazine in the clip until it clicked into place. Fearing that John might have heard, he quickly checked on his partner again. He was oblivious.

Sammy then pulled the slide back and released, loading the first round in the chamber. If John asked him later what that sound was, he could brush it off as dropping something onto the floor of his Jeep. He engaged the safety, then slowly replaced the gun in the glove box. What his friend didn't know couldn't hurt him.

Sammy quickly retrieved their folding chairs and folding table and hiked back to their camp. John had just finished getting things arranged to his liking.

"Wow, this is an incredible place! I could just sit and enjoy this all weekend." said John.

"Don't go getting all comfortable just yet, buddy. It's late afternoon, but we've still got hours of daylight left. Aren't you itching to be the first to find that new cache?" asked Sammy.

"Actually, now that we're out here, yeah, I'm stoked to go find it. Let's grab a little wood for tonight, then head out."

In short order, they had a nice pile of branches and a few larger pieces of wood sitting near the ring of rocks. They each got out their handheld GPS units and synced them up so that they had the same cache points. Putting on their waist packs, they set out toward the first cache of the weekend.

The forest was denser than they had imagined it would be. It made hiking slower, which meant that they may not be able to make it to this new cache they wanted to find before dark. Every so often, they would pull out their GPS units to make sure that they were still heading in the right direction. The sun was mostly behind them, as they were walking in a northeast direction from their camp, but it was still hot on their necks. Sammy pushed through a thicket of small trees and brambles as he forged a trail toward their goal.

"I don't recall you mentioning that we would be trail-busting to get to this cache," complained John.

"Where's your sense of adventure? This is all part of the excitement!" replied Sammy.

"Adventure, sure. Getting slapped in the face with tree branches? Not so much."

They paused in the middle of a small cluster of trees for a break. Sammy got out his GPS unit to check how far they were from the cache while John took a long drink from his water bottle. The afternoon sun, while still hot, was dropping slowly in the western sky. Evening would be here soon, and they knew they needed to find the cache soon or else they would have to try looking for it tomorrow.

"You ready for more adventure?" asked Sammy. "We're close now. And time's running out. Let's go, muchacho."

They took off again in search of their prey, such as it was. They both had their GPS units out, tracking their progress. They emerged from the woods into a large clearing, hundreds of feet across and roughly rectangular. Tall tan grasses swayed in the gentle breeze. They started across the open field.

"Hold up, Sam."

"What for?"

"It's around here, this side of the clearing."

"Are you sure? My GPS still shows that we've got a few hundred yards to go, which would put it on the other side of the field."

"Force an update on your unit. Then you'll see what I see."

Sammy complied, and his unit recalculated its position with the satellites orbiting thousands of miles overhead.

"Sweet! Let's get searching."

8

Everyone's got their own method of searching for a geocache once they get close to the location. Some people are methodical and others are just willy-nilly. Some can get 'feelings' about what direction it might be in while others virtually trip over the cache, having been born under a lucky star. After many times being out in the boonies, Sammy and John had developed a method that worked pretty well for them in a short period of time.

They each did their own thing.

Fortunately, they each did a *different* thing, which resulted in one or the other finding the cache in short order. John, being the more structured of the two, often did a self-described search pattern. From where he was on the edge of the clearing, he started his methodical search tree by tree, convinced that it was the most logical place to hide a cache.

Sammy, on the other hand, was more free-wheeling, and as such took a different tack. Being a few dozen feet out in the clearing, he surveyed their surroundings, evaluating the best locations for hiding a cache, and took into account John's chosen approach to check the trees. Grabbing a long branch from the ground nearby, he started sweeping through the grasses, poking at the ground occasionally.

John slowly wound his way around the trees, looking them up and down, trying to find a small nook or cranny where someone could hide a small canister or bottle. They may even be looking for something as small as a pill bottle, so he took his time trying not to miss the small places. Sammy wasn't having any better luck out in the field. There wasn't anything except the grass to hide the cache, and he doubted that someone would just leave a small plastic container out there as the cache. Too easy to break if someone stepped on it, and too easy to move to another location in this large field. All of that meant it would be too difficult for the person who placed it to maintain it properly, especially way out here.

After nearly ten minutes of searching, they reconvened near the edge of the woods. Sammy dragged his GPS unit out again and rechecked the coordinates to make sure they were looking in the right place. John rescanned the trees and the ground for what felt like the hundredth time. Then something caught his eye.

He kept staring at the ground as he walked over near the base of a tall white pine tree. He stopped, looked at the ground all around, then returned his gaze to the spot he noticed before. Mulling things over in his mind a few seconds more, he knelt down and started digging at the ground with his hands. The dirt gave way a little too easily in his hands, and he started excavating a small hole. A few inches down, his fingers felt something cold and hard.

"Sammy!" yelled John over his shoulder.

Sammy had been focused on his GPS unit and hadn't noticed what John was doing. Looking up, he was surprised to find his friend hard at work digging a hole. With his bare hands.

Hurrying over to his friend, Sammy knelt down and helped him dig out around the emerging container. After a few moments,

Sammy tried lifting out the metal container. It released from the dirt, and he set it between them. It was a dull green ammo case the military used. On one side was spray-painted a large black "X".

They looked at each other with satisfaction and anticipation. Neither of them wanted to end the mystery of their search, yet they both wanted to see what was inside and to mark the log book as the first to find the cache.

John finally broke the stalemate and undid the latch. He flipped back the cover and looked inside. The shadow he cast combined with the still-bright sunshine in his eyes made it look like the case was empty. He reached in, feeling around the cold steel case. His fingers encountered a thick square piece of paper that was smooth on one side and slightly rough on the other side. He quickly pulled it out and realized what it was: a photograph.

"Is that it?" asked Sammy.

"That can't be it," replied John. He set the picture down on the ground, grabbed the ammo box, tipped it upside down and shook it. Tiny pieces of dirt fell to ground. John slumped down on his legs, practically dropping the ammo box back on the ground.

"Are you sure we found the right cache?" asked John. "I mean, they aren't normally buried like that one was. In fact, I've never had to dig a cache out. Have you?"

Sammy pulled out his GPS to recheck the coordinates. "Nope, never have. Coordinates are right."

"What in the world..." John threw his hands up in frustration. They both looked around the area, hoping to see where the actual geocache was that they should have found. John picked up the picture again.

"Well, might as well take a look at what was in the box."

They both looked at the picture. Then they looked even closer. Then they looked at each other, and back to the picture.

"What the hell is that?" asked Sammy in disbelief.

They were staring at a photo. Of themselves. Taken a couple of hours ago. At their camp.

9

They continued to stare at the picture of themselves taken just hours before. The photo was taken when they were setting up camp and unloading their Jeeps. John was completing his tent setup as Sammy was standing at his passenger door looking at something.

"How...? Who...?" Sammy stammered, running his hands through his hair.

"I don't know. It obviously wasn't us."

"Thank you, Sherlock," retorted Sammy.

Silence fell between the two as John continued to stare at the picture while Sammy paced around trying to make sense of things. John noticed that the picture was taken from in the woods, not out in the open, which would have helped conceal whoever took the picture. The big question was, who knew that they were coming out here?

"Did we pass anyone as we drove in?" asked John.

"Nope. Don't remember anyone following us either."

"What about the hot chick at the gas station? You were chatting her up before I got in there. Did you tell her anything?"

Sammy thought back to Jamie, her eyes, her curves. Did he inadvertently give her the location where they would be? He was known to say dumb things around beautiful young women, and this time might have been no exception.

"I don't think I did." replied Sammy

"Aw, crud!"

"Hey, hey, watch that language, God-boy."

"Shut up, okay? This is a serious problem. Someone is stalking us. You find that funny?" asked John.

Sammy chuckled a little at John's reaction. He'd had a chance to process things, and now he didn't feel like it was as serious as he once did.

"Actually, now I do, just a little. So what if it was her? Are you really afraid that she's going to track us down and kill us? Or lead us to our deaths?"

"I don't know what to think, because we're still guessing. What if it wasn't her but instead was someone else getting us wrapped up in their sick little game?"

Sammy thought about that for a minute. It was true they didn't know who could have put that there. But it was also true the only person that either of them had talked to about their plans was Jamie. And she didn't strike Sammy as the homicidal type.

"So, what other information do we have at this point? We only have the coordinates for this location and a picture that was taken a couple hours ago."

John had to admit that there wasn't anything else that they could point to as evidence for something or someone. The only thing they had was the picture.

The picture.

John studied the image again, trying to determine if he could learn anything else about the person who took it. Nothing else jumped out at him after spending minutes looking at every inch.

"Find anything useful in your pictorial study?" asked Sammy.

"Nada. Looks like this was just a wild goose chase for us." Almost as an afterthought, John flipped the picture over and glanced at the back. Writing caught his eye. "Hey! I think I found a clue."

Sammy had been wandering around in the open field, but now jogged back to where John had been sitting. John handed the picture to him and told him to look on the back. He read the message.

Surprise! Follow me to find out who I am.

Below the message was a set of coordinates. Sammy let out a low whistle. "Where do think they lead?" he asked.

"Seriously? You're actually thinking of following the coordinates?"

"It's the only lead we've got, muchacho. You have any better ideas?"

"Sure. Let's turn this in to the police, let them handle it."

"What are they gonna do?" asked Sammy. "They don't have any more than we do to go on. It isn't a high priority for them to do a handwriting analysis, the picture could have been made from any number of dozens, if not hundreds of cameras. Besides, there isn't anything nefarious being done at this point that would warrant them getting involved. They would probably say to leave it and go home, and I don't want to do that. Do you?"

John sat and thought more about everything that had happened in the last few minutes. He couldn't point to anything that would cause the police or anyone else to do an investigation. Nonetheless, he still had a bad feeling about following the coordinates. They didn't map it out ahead of time, so they could lead anywhere. What if the coordinates were far enough away that they needed to drive there? Would they still follow them?

As John continued to wrestle with what to do, Sammy had made up his mind – he was already plugging the new coordinates into his GPS unit to find out how far away the next cache was from their current location. Zooming out on the screen, it looked to be within a quarter-mile from where they were.

"So, you comin' or stayin'?" asked Sammy.

John looked up to see Sammy walking away from him through the open field.

"You're following them?" asked John incredulously.

"Only way to find anything out," Sammy yelled back.

"Off to the guillotine," John muttered to himself. He got up and jogged through the field to catch up with Sammy. As they walked, John plugged the coordinates into his GPS as well. They always had the same coordinates in each of their machines as backups for each other. It was possible that one of them could suddenly malfunction, they could lose one of them, or any number of other oddities. Because they were electronic devices, they also carried the analog equivalent with them as well: a compass and terrain map.

They closed the distance quickly to the next cache. This one wasn't as difficult to locate as the first one. Sammy found a hard plastic tube with a soft plastic cap wedged in the crook of a tree. Inside was a small piece of paper.

You're getting warmer.

Another set of coordinates greeted them with the message. Sammy entered them into his GPS unit. John looked up at the fading light in the sky. He would have to play to Sammy's nature if he was going to get some common-sense thinking from him.

"I know," John said, "you're eager to find out where this all leads, and while I'm not the most cooperative on that front at the moment, I'm in agreement with you on getting to the bottom of things. However, we're rapidly losing what little daylight we have. Why don't we head back to camp, get a good meal and a decent night's sleep, and then hit it hard tomorrow?"

Sammy stopped and looked around, noticing for the first time just how much light they had lost from when they had started until now. He struggled with putting the adventure on hold, the fully-charged headlamp in his waistpack screaming to be used. Reluctantly, he agreed with his friend's thinking.

"Yeah, that sounds good. We'll regroup and solve this thing tomorrow."

They both silently hoped that whoever took the picture didn't do something to their camp.

10

Finding their way back didn't take nearly as long as tracking down the geocaches. Halfway back to camp, the forest blocked out the remaining rays of sunlight and forced them to don their headlamps. This was not the place to take a chance on twisting an ankle or breaking a leg or arm. Once back, they combed through their gear but found nothing indicating that anyone had been there. Likewise with their vehicles.

Satisfied, they started a fire and got their meals prepared. As they sat around the fire eating, they were both consumed with the events of the day. The evening was beautiful, with a nearly fully moon rising and a clear sky that allowed the brilliance of a million stars to poke through the blackness. The dancing flames mesmerized them, having a hypnotic-like hold on their eyes.

"How set are you on continuing to follow the coordinates?" asked John, continuing to stare into the flames. Sammy didn't answer right away, causing John to look up at him. "Well?"

"I think we should," Sammy answered. He continued to focus on the bright embers at the base of the fire, the image consuming him like the fire consumed the wood.

"What do you think we'll find? Anything?"

"Probably just a stupid dog turd or something. Somebody's idea of a weird joke."

"Then why even continue with it?"

"Because, John," answered Sammy. He locked eyes with him across the the fire. "It's why we come out here. It's why we put so much energy into this geocaching thing. It's the adventure! The not knowing what's in the next cache, around the next bend, or over the next hill. It's the thrill of discovering something that only a few people have or will ever find. That's what keeps us going, what gives us the fuel to push forward when others give up. That's why we'll get up early tomorrow morning and make a beeline for the next cache. It's the adventure, bro!"

John was stunned with his mini-speech. Never had his friend put things so succinctly, so perfect. All he could do was stare back in awe.

Sammy noticed that his speech had struck a nerve with John, and his mouth quivered just a little, then began to form a small smirk. "Or, you know, maybe I just planned this whole thing as a prank on you."

"W-what? You did what?"

Sammy threw his head back in delight, laughing hard. "Oh! You're the best, man. I love it when I get you."

John couldn't help but laugh at his gullibility. Sammy was known for pranking people, but John doubted that he could have pulled this one off.

"You're right, though, you know," said John after the laughter died off. "We're out here for adventure. And really, nothing yet has been that bad. All right, you've convinced me. Let's go track it down."

"All right, man! Let's do it. Shoot, if I'd a known it was going to be that easy, I would have made that speech while we were at the second cache."

John threw his plastic fork at his friend in mock anger, and they both shared another laugh. They cleaned up dinner and secured their vehicles in the dwindling firelight, then turned in for the night.

* * * * *

The camera zoomed in on them as they sat down around the fire.
Click! Click!
"Better to have the pictures, just in case."
The heavier man ate quickly while the skinnier, darker-skinned one ate more slowly. No conversation happened between them for quite a while. Then they looked at each other. Could they have heard something?
"Nah, what would they hear anyway? Probably just a deer or somethin."
Now the two of them shared a laugh.
Click!
"Perfect."
The heavier man threw something at the skinnier one, then they laughed again. They got up, did a few things, then crawled into their tents.
"Sleep tight, purdy boys."

* * *

The morning began with a colorful sunrise. Both Sammy and John sat in their low chairs facing the eastern sky, mugs of coffee warming their hands. They had moved to the other side of their Jeeps in order to better watch the sun rise above the treeline.

Waking up early in the morning on most days was not a positive experience for John. He was not a morning person, especially on work days, but when he was out camping and geocaching it didn't feel quite so bad. Sammy on the other hand was used to getting up early to start his day. Landscaping was best done in the daylight, and during the summer months it was important to use them all, especially in the northern latitudes of Minnesota. He took pity on John and made coffee while John was still stumbling out of his tent.

"Wow, this is truly beautiful," exclaimed John.

"Agreed."

The silence between them resumed as they continued to take in the sunrise. The birds sang their morning tunes, waking up the entire forest to another day in wooded bliss.

Draining their mugs, they returned the chairs to the previous night's locations, then went through the usual morning equipment check. Within twenty minutes, they were loaded up with gear, food and water, ready to head out to the coordinates that were on the piece of paper from the last cache they visited yesterday.

"Onward to adventure," said Sammy as he slapped his friend on the back and headed off into the woods.

11

The morning dew left their boots wet while the crisp air invigorated their steps. The bright sunshine of the early hours held an air of hope, of goodwill. They marched toward their target in silence, both wondering what they would find at the next cache. Along the way they stirred up a doe from her resting spot in a thicket; she moved too quickly for either of them to snap a picture.

The intensity of the sun was just beginning to bear down on them as they reached the next cache. This one wasn't hidden nearly as well as the last one and they found it within minutes of arriving in the designated area. This cache was like the last with a short encouraging note and a set of coordinates. Their expectations lessening by the hour that this would be anything of interest in the end, they set off in search of the next cache.

An hour later they located the next cache. This too was hidden very poorly, and contained the same ingredients of a message and coordinates. As Sammy entered the next set of coordinates into his GPS unit, John sat down on a fallen log for a brief rest.

"All right, I've entertained this series of caches for long enough," declared John. "This is the last one. If nothing good comes from this one, I'm calling it quits. We didn't come here for the run around, we came to find some caches."

Sammy exhaled loudly and looked up at the bright midday sky. He never liked to admit defeat, but he also liked to have a purpose to what he was doing. This didn't appear to have any purpose other than to annoy the one trying to follow the coordinates. "Yeah, you're probably right."

John looked up at Sammy from his log sofa.

"What?" asked Sammy. "Don't look at me like that. I'll admit that this ONE time you might have a point."

John was a little surprised at his friend's admission. "Whoa, partner! You going soft on me?"

"Whatever. So we're calling it? This one has to be something good, or we end it and move on to the other caches?"

"Sounds good to me. Let's hit it."

Sammy took a long drink from his canteen while John plugged in the coordinates, then they headed out to what they both figured was the last cache on the wild goose chase.

The morning slipped away into afternoon as the friends made their way through the forest. They silently noted that this would-be last cache was much further away from the last than any of the previous caches. As they continued on, they entered a portion of the forest that was much more dense than other sections they had been in. The trees were larger in diameter and much closer in proximity to each other, and the branch and leaf density was more intense. A noticeable decrease in sunlight made it seem as though evening was suddenly upon them as they forged deeper into the old-growth forest.

As they did on other geocache hunts from time to time, John and Sammy stopped to get their bearings, take a drink, and generally rest. It took a few minutes before John noticed something missing.

"Do you hear that?" asked John.

Sammy broke from reviewing his GPS unit and listened intently for what his friend obviously heard.

"What am I listening for?"

"You can't tell?"

Sammy strained to hear something, anything.

"I don't hear a flippin' thing."

"Exactly. Doesn't that strike you as odd?"

"Definitely. Old-growth woods like this are usually teaming with life. That's a little disconcerting, even for me."

"I for one don't want to stick around to find out why. We're close now. Let's find it and call it a day."

They headed deeper into the dense woods, keeping an eye on their GPS units. With the increased density, their progress slowed, and it took nearly a half-hour to get to the area where the cache was supposed to be. All of the previous caches had been in, on, or near the ground, so they began their search low. In short order, they realized that this cache would be more difficult to locate, as there were numerous places to hide a cache; the smaller it was, the more difficult it was to find.

After nearly another half-hour of searching, Sammy discovered a small plastic tube hidden in a hole in an old tree. As he took it out, he could feel something rattling around inside. John joined him as he stood next to the large dead oak tree that housed the cache. The tube was clear plastic about six inches long and a couple inches in diameter with black plastic caps at both ends. Paper encircled the inside of the tube which prevented them from seeing what was inside.

Sammy pulled off one of the black caps and tipped the tube into his hand. A rusty old iron key dropped into his hand.

"What the hell?" exclaimed Sammy.

"Not what I expected. Is there anything else?"

Sammy quickly looked inside the tube. "Nope."

"So, what does the key mean?"

"Beats the hell out of me. Maybe this isn't the right cache. Let's look around, see if we can find another one."

For the next forty-five minutes they scoured the area, even climbing up a few smaller trees to check from different vantage points. Frustrated, they each took a seat on a large dead tree that had fallen over. As the afternoon wore on, the minimal light began to fade even more. They would soon have to head back to camp, or at least move into a less dense portion of the forest.

"Let me see the tube," said John.

Sammy handed it over as John got out his headlamp from his waist pack. Turning on the light, he peered into the tube. Reaching in he pulled out the paper.

"You know, sometimes it's best to check things thoroughly rather than just rushing to bad conclusions."

John handed the paper over to Sammy. Sammy read it, then hung his head. More coordinates.

"Wow, I'm an ass. I'm sorry for making us look all over, again."

"I'm not happy about it either, but at least we've got something more than just a key. But I don't like this. It feels like a setup of some kind."

"It's just a key. What could happen?"

John thought about that question for a few moments. The only difference between this cache and all the others was the addition of the key. And all of those had been benign enough.

"I know. But sometimes I get this gut feeling that something isn't right, and that's what I've got now."

"Look, I know that you haven't been too excited about this geocaching trip thus far, but I at least want to find out what this all leads to. We've invested so much time already, might as well try to get some payoff from it."

Without waiting for his friend's response, Sammy punched in the coordinates from the paper into his GPS unit and stood to go. John sighed as he stood. "Fine, but I'm on record declaring this a bad idea."

"Duly noted. Let's finish this thing."

12

    If it were possible, it seemed to Sammy and John that the forest got even more dense as they continued their quest to finish the series of cache coordinates. As they picked their way through the undergrowth, the light continued to wane. More than once, John voiced his opinion that they should call it quits and head back to camp before it got pitch dark and they needed to use their headlamps. Walking in the woods was one thing, but it became much more difficult to navigate in the dark. A tree that, in the daylight, would have distinctive features, easily became just another tree at night. Not to mention the higher probability of tripping and falling, and potentially twisting an ankle – or worse.

    And then it was in front of them. While they were watching where they were walking and checking their GPS units, they had come upon a small clearing in the dense forest. Sunlight poured through the opening in the canopy above and created streams of light that shimmered as insects flew through them. At the far edge of the clearing sat a small building covered with green moss. The scene looked like a fairy tale or a painting by Thomas Kinkade.

After taking in the beautiful late afternoon scene, they approached the small old building. At the peak of the roof was an ornate iron cross, the deteriorating wooden shakes were damp and covered with moss. The single window on one side had surprisingly escaped the hands of vandals and of the weather. Facing the duo was a large arched doorway with two doors that each filled one half of the opening, which itself ate up over half of the exterior wall. Wrapped around the iron handles on the doors was a length of new silver chain with an equally new padlock securely fastened.

"Looks like we've made it to the end of the line," said Sammy.

"Let's hurry up and check this out. We're running out of daylight."

Sammy pulled out the key they had found at the last cache a number of hours ago. Without hesitation, he inserted the key in the padlock and twisted. With a discernible click, the lock snapped open. Sammy quickly undid the lock and chain and tossed it in a pile on the ground. He grasped a door handle and pulled, opening the door to their latest exploit.

The interior of the church was as run down as the exterior. Short wooden pews claimed the center of the main area; they were rotting and covered with moss, the ceiling having begun to give way in a few places. At the front of the church was a raised stage. A single wooden pulpit stood off to one side of the stage, and against the back wall was another pew; both had seen better days. The floor was rough-hewn boards, and the rafters were small logs stripped of bark – probably right from these woods.

Despite its obvious run-down condition, it was in fairly good shape overall. It didn't appear that the building had been used recently, for church services or anything else. Thin lines of light poked through the holes in the roof and the single window provided enough light to make out the general condition of the interior.

"Great, now what are we supposed to do?" asked John.

"I'll bet there's a clue here somewhere." replied Sammy. He moved off to start exploring the pews.

Disgusted, John took a slow look around the interior, hoping that Sammy would grow tired quickly so they could start heading back.

"What are you doing just standing there?"

"There's nothing here, Sammy. This was probably it, just to show us a really old church that was probably used by loggers a century ago."

"Look, I know you want to get going, and I will. Just give me a few more minutes to look around, k?"

John huffed in agreement, then slowly started to look around more closely. The pews had intricate carvings on the sides, full of religious connotations. From underneath one of the pews John extracted an old hymnal. The paper was brittle from exposure to the elements, and easily tore as he flipped through the pages.

Sammy had reached the front of the pews without finding anything. He looked up and searched the dark room to locate his friend. In his scan of the room, he noticed something sitting on the top of the pulpit on the stage. Intrigued, he stepped up on the stage and walked the few steps to stand behind the pulpit. Looking completely out of place sat a brand new Bible. He stared at it quizzically, shocked to find anything new in this ramshackle building.

"Hey John, come here."

John looked up at the stage.

"What, did you find another set of coordinates?" asked John sarcastically.

Sammy started flipping through the Bible, still amazed that it was here.

"Who would have left this here, and why?" he asked to himself.

"What? I couldn't hear you."
Sammy looked up at his friend across the room.
"I said, who-"
And then he was gone.

13

In John's mind, the previous few seconds replayed in slow motion. His friend was about to repeat what he had said, and then he dropped behind the pulpit. Gone.

"Sammy?"

He continued to stare at the pulpit, not believing his eyes and ears. He started moving towards the stage as fear began to well up within him.

"Sammy!"

As he landed on the stage, he heard a loud snap and felt movement in the floor through his shoes. He turned to look at the pulpit in time to see a trap door quickly close in the floor directly behind the pulpit. The Bible remained open where Sammy was paging through it.

"Holy shit! SAMMY!"

John dove to the floor and slid to a stop with his face hovering over the now-closed trap door.

"SAMMY! Can you hear me?"

He strained to hear something, anything through the thick old wood. Then, faintly:

"John?"

Relief flooded his body, yet he remained as tense as ever. Was he okay? Where was he? How did it happen? How could he get out?

"Sammy, are you hurt? How far did you fall?"

Silence. Then a scream of pain pierced John's ears.

"Sammy! What's happening?"

"It's okay. I think I broke my leg when I hit bottom."

John dropped his head and smacked the wood floor. That's not what they needed right now.

"Was that what the scream was for?"

"Yeah," Sammy replied weakly. "I can't see shit down here."

"Don't you have your pack? Your headlamp should be in there."

Silence. John imagined his friend checking his body and the area around him for the small pack.

"Nope. Must have gotten ripped off during my fall. Ahh! Damn, that hurts. Dude, you gotta get me outta here."

"I'm on it!"

John leapt to his feet and scanned the room. He searched for something, anything to try to wedge under the trap door. He whipped around and looked at what was on the small stage. There, standing next to the rotting pew, was a candle stand about five feet tall. The heavily tarnished brass looked like it had seen better days, but was still solid as John banged it on the floor and a low ring emanated from the pole. He managed to pull the pole out of the loose base, and set to work trying to pry open the trap door to get to Sammy.

As he worked to open the door, a deep voice boomed inside the church, scaring him. "John!"

He dropped the pole and immediately looked around, sure he would find someone else there with him.

The church was empty.

14

"John!"

He looked around the church and saw no one. The voice had seemingly come from all around him. Combined with his fear for his friend, his intimidation grew and he slowly lowered himself to the floor, looking up at the ceiling expectantly. Swallowing hard, he felt foolish, but went ahead nonetheless.

"God?"

Deep laughter filled his ears. Joyful, mirthful, arrogant laughter. It grated on him.

"Yes," replied the voice, "I suppose that I am at this point."

Unsure what to do next, he said nothing but waited for what would come next. The silence that followed the voice was nearly as loud in John's head as the voice was.

"Looking for your friend?"

John nodded, still not ready to speak again.

"Sammy is okay...fer now."

Anger welled up in him in an instant. "Did you do this? Where is he?" yelled John at the air as he stood up in defiance.

"He's below the church."

"I know that. What I want to know is why, and how I can get him out."

The voice ignored his demands.

"I want to thank you for playin' along with the caches. I didn't expect to have someone so soon."

"So it was you. What was the point of all of this?"

"I like games. You like games, John?"

His anger increased at the use of his name, as if they were friends. He tried to keep himself in check. Getting out of control wouldn't help his friend.

"I'll ask you again: how can I get him out?"

"I don't think you in a position ta make demands, do you? Now, answer my question."

John considered, if only for a brief moment, just leaving the church. But, he knew Sammy wouldn't do it if things were reversed, no matter how much he wanted to. If it would mean that he could get to help his friend sooner, he could play along for a while. A short while. He started exploring inside the church, looking for anything that would give him a clue as to who the voice belonged to.

"What are you looking for, John?"

"Sure, I like games," he replied.

"Oh good, I thought you was ignoring my question. What kind of games do you like, John? Do you like adventure games?"

He had searched up and down the pews on both sides and began looking underneath them.

"Looking for clues, John? I don't think you'll find anythin' down there."

He got up and looked up at the rotting ceiling. Then he spotted it, right above the entrance. A small black camera staring back at him.

"Ah, very good, detective. So nice to meet you."

"Why not come out of hiding, coward?"

"And ruin the fun I'm having? I don't think so."

He turned away in disgust and went back to the stage where he resumed working on the trap door. The floor boards started to split and splinter as he worked the end of the pole into the tiny gap.

"You'll be here fer days tryin' to get that open. And that won't happen with the steel bars underneath the door."

He kept working for a few seconds more, then stopped. He stood there, considering his options and waited to see if the voice would add anything else. Minutes of silence passed.

"So how do I get him out?"

More silence. A fresh round of anger began to rise in his belly. More minutes passed in silence. Frustrated, John threw the pole at the camera above the door. It missed by mere inches and fell to the floor with a loud crash.

"Temper, temper, John."

"SHUT UP! SHUT UP!"

"I'm the one in control here. You ain't answered my question."

Breathing hard with frustration and anger, he searched his rage-clouded mind for the question the voice had asked. Finally he remembered.

"Yeah, I like adventure games."

"Very good! I hate repeatin' myself, so you've won the privilege of asking me any question you want and I'll answer honestly. Make it a good one, John."

He sat down on the edge of the stage and contemplated what he should ask. He knew that it would have to be about Sammy, but what exactly? He also knew that it would have to be something that couldn't be answered simply with a *yes* or *no*.

"What do I have to do to save my friend?"

Once again, silence permeated the air. John struggled to maintain his composure as the seconds turned into minutes.

"That's a very selfless question, John. Admirable."

He waited for the voice to continue. He started contemplating what he would do if he didn't get an answer.

"Do you have a flashlight, John?"

"What about answering my question?"

"Patience. I'm tryin' to help you, even if you don't believe it."

He took a deep breath, attempting to calm himself and not lose out on the chance to save Sammy.

"Yes, I have a headlamp."

"Excellent! You DO like adventure games and you've come prepared. I like that in my players."

"Splendid. What do I have to do?"

"Oh, now John, you don't have to repeat your questions. You need to work on patience. Patience is a virtue, you know."

"Look, I'm tired of this evasive, twenty-questions game you're playing. You proved your point, you're in charge. I just want to help my friend."

He flopped down in a pew.

"Please."

Outside, a bird called its evening song. John remembered how late it was when they got there, and now this drawn out conversation with a hidden person playing an annoying question game had made him forget just how much time had passed. It would be a long trek back to camp, if he could get his friend out safely from wherever he was.

"Go to these coordinates."

John jumped at the sound of the voice, having been lost in his thoughts. He ripped out his GPS unit and quickly entered the numbers the voice rattled off to him. The GPS wouldn't update the distance until he got back outside with a clear shot at the satellites orbiting the Earth.

"Your friend is there."

15

"Why are you doing this?"

John slowly scanned the ceiling, waiting for an answer that would never come.

"ANSWER ME!"

Only the evening crickets answered his inquiry. He quickly realized that he wouldn't be having any more conversations with the disembodied voice. He climbed onto the stage again and knelt by the trap door that he failed to pry open earlier.

"Sammy! Sammy, can you hear me?"

John pressed his ear to the floor, straining to hear. It was difficult to make out, but he could hear his friend.

"What's going on up there, bro?"

John exhaled a sigh of relief; his friend was still alive. But he needed to get moving or he might not stay that way.

"Sammy! I think I've got a way to get you out. I need to go to another set of coordinates. Hang tight, buddy, I'll get you out."

Again, he pressed his ear to the floor, awaiting a response. The seconds ticked by without a sound from below.

"SAMMY!"

He listened again, but the beating of his heart in his ears made it harder to hear anything, especially if it was faint. His mind started to reel in unpleasant directions.

"Go," came the weak reply. "Hurry."

John lingered for a few moments, then got up and collected himself. He dropped off the stage, then turned around and looked at the wall at the back of the stage. The last rays of sunlight pierced the single window on the wall and shone bright orange on the cross that was anchored to the wall. He stood, transfixed by the sight. Briefly, he bowed his head and said a silent prayer. The forest honored the moment by remaining in silence with him.

He looked up again at the cross, determination set on his face. He pulled out the headlamp from his pack and strapped it around his head. The LEDs came to life and he headed out the door. Outside, he waited for a minute as his GPS unit located and locked onto the satellites that were overhead. With the new coordinates in place, the arrow on the LCD screen pointed the way forward.

Hiking through the woods at night was a much slower proposition than in the daylight. It was much easier to miss a root sticking out of the ground that could be tripped over, twisting an ankle. Or bash a knee on a rock. Or fall into a shallow hole. The list went on and on. And he didn't even want to think about the animals that he could come across.

After twenty minutes of picking his way through the dense forest, he checked the GPS unit to see how he had progressed. Surprisingly, he found that he was closer than he thought. He adjusted his heading and pushed forward with renewed vigor. Thoughts of his friend swirled in his head. He had to get him out of there and get help.

Just a few minutes later John stepped into a small clearing. He stood at the edge and swiveled his head around, swiping the beam of his headlamp over the area. As he moved from right to left, the ground rose quickly in a hill, and gently tapered off again as he continued to the left. In the middle of the hill he caught sight of some old lumber. Scanning it further with the headlamp, he found that it was boards nailed across an opening.

Interested, he closed the distance to investigate. As he got close, he could read faint white letters on a board fastened at the top of the opening. *Regis Mine.* The other boards were obviously there to keep people out, and one of them even had those words along with the skull and cross bones symbol.

John took out his GPS unit again and checked the coordinates. He was right on top of the place the disembodied voice said he should go. He looked around again to be sure there wasn't anything else obvious that he might have missed. Seeing nothing, he turned back to the mine entrance. He would need to remove a couple of the boards so he could get through. Grasping one at shoulder height, he braced his leg on the wood frame outlining the entrance. With all of his strength he pulled as hard as he could.

The boards weren't nailed in nearly as strongly as he anticipated. The combined force of the yank with his arms and the push of his leg easily dislodged the board and he sailed backward, landing with a thud on his back on the mossy ground, board still clutched in his hands. He laid on the ground for a minute, letting the small pain and shock subside. He chuckled to himself as he imagined Sammy would be in hysterics if he were here to witness John's triumphant removal of the board.

Getting up, he tossed the board aside and went back to the entrance. More careful the second time around, he found the other boards equally as ready to give up their hold. He cleared the entrance in short order, took a deep breath, and plunged into the heavy darkness of the mine.

16

As soon as he landed, Sammy was sure he had broken something. Lying there in the dark on the cold ground, he remembered something that his skydiving instructor had once said.

It's not the fall that will kill you. It's the sudden stop at the end.

He continued to lie in silence, his brain running a diagnostic on the rest of his body, taking stock of what still worked and what was damaged. He thought he faintly heard noise above him. Then, sounding muffled and distant:

"SAMMY! Can you hear me?"

Was that really John? He tried to reply, but his voice didn't immediately respond. Forcing harder, he managed to croak out a reply.

"John?"

No reply came immediately, and he wondered if perhaps he didn't dream the voice.

"Sammy, are you hurt? How far did you fall?"

Sammy was surprised at his relief that he didn't imagine his friend's voice. Checking both of his arms, he found that they were fine. He pushed himself into a seated position on the ground, then moved to check his legs. His left leg and foot appeared okay, and he slowly rotated his ankle to check for range of motion. It was a little sore, but otherwise felt solid to him. Then he moved to his right leg and attempted to do the same check.

"AAAHHH! Sonofabitch!" he yelled out.

He grimaced and gritted his teeth against the waves of pain that rolled through his leg and body. He could barely keep himself in a sitting position, nausea following on the heels of the pain. He felt like he might black out.

"Sammy! What's happening?"

He took audible breaths through gritted teeth as the pain subsided. Gingerly he touched his shin and ankle, each press sending small lightning bolts of fresh pain. This was not what he needed.

"It's okay. I think I broke my leg when I hit bottom."

Trying hard not to bump any part of his lower leg, Sammy found he could still bend his knee, which also appeared to have survived the impact. He gently lowered his leg back down but still managed to hit a nerve just right which took his breath away.

"Was that what the scream was for?" John asked from somewhere above.

"Yeah," Sammy replied weakly. "I can't see shit down here."

"Don't you have your pack? Your headlamp should be in there."

He hadn't given a thought to anything else other than his own body. Instinctively, his hands went to his waist. Nothing. He couldn't feel the nylon belt or the plastic buckle anywhere around his waist.

"Shit."

With his limited reach, he tried to feel around where he was sitting. Pawing at the ground with his calloused hands, all he felt were a few small rocks and dust. Wherever it got to, he probably would never find it in the dark and with a bum leg.

"Nope. Must have gotten ripped off during my fall," replied Sammy. He tried to readjust his sitting position, and jostled his right leg a little. "AHH! Damn, that hurts. Dude, you gotta get me outta here."

"I'm on it!"

Sammy was left in silent darkness once again to contemplate his next move.

17

"Maybe I'm too adventurous for my own good."

Sammy decided to throw himself his very own pity party. Very often he would be the one working to cheer up one of his friends, trying to get them to look on the bright side, not give up, and so on. But it was pretty difficult to do the same thing for himself in a situation like this. What bright side was there to this?

Above him, Sammy could have sworn that he heard voices. And not just of his friend either. Unfortunately, it was so slight that after straining to hear for a couple of minutes, he gave up. He couldn't make anything out, and it wasn't helping his present situation.

Concentrating once again on his surroundings, he decided that he should try to see if he could move around and maybe get himself out. Who knew how long it would take John to find him, and Sammy was not one to just let life happen to him. Taking care not to hit or otherwise jar his right leg, he pulled his left leg into his body and rocked forward with his right leg still stretched out in front of him. Balanced on his left foot, he began to bounce to gain some momentum so that he could stand up. After a couple of bounces he pushed hard with his left leg up to a standing position.

His head hit the rock ceiling with a thud, his teeth banged together hard.

"Fuck!"

As quickly as he shot up, he folded over and crumpled down on the ground again. On the way down, he jammed his right leg on the ground, causing a fresh jolt of intense pain to rock his body. His head and left shoulder smacked the hard ground, nearly knocking him out. He screamed out in pain and anger, rolling slowly over onto his back. For a long time he laid flat out, moaning and waiting for the pain to lessen.

"I don't want to do that again."

He sat up again, his head still hurting along with the rest of his body. Now that he'd had a chance to settle down from all of the events, he could feel the various aches coming from all over his body and joints. Wherever he was, the ceiling was obviously lower than he figured. He maneuvered onto his knees so that he could start to feel around the pitch black space.

He started to slowly move forward in a three-legged lumber. He was careful to keep his right leg as stationary as possible, but it still caused him pain whenever he shifted his weight forward onto his arms and pulled his legs forward. As he moved his hands forward, he would sweep each arm around to see if he could find anything that would help provide him some clues and keep him safe: the edge of the wall, a hole in the floor, something that he could use as a splint to keep his leg set straight.

After a few feet, his hand closed around a nice sized rock. It was too small to be used for defensive purposes, but he thought he might be able to tell just how big the space was by listening to the sound of it bouncing along when he threw it. Pushing himself back up onto his left knee, he tossed the stone in front of him. Barely breathing, he waited for it to hit the ground. He was hoping that it would hit a wall and bounce back toward him.

What he heard made him get a confused look on his face. There was nothing. No sound at all from the stone he threw. He felt around again on the floor and found another stone about the same size. Again he threw the stone, but harder this time. The same result greeted him.

"What the hell?"

He started to lumber forward again, but then stopped. It could be that he was on a ledge, and that the stones fell so far down that he wouldn't have heard the noise. But where was the edge? Carefully, he shuffled forward, his hands searching wildly as he went along.

Suddenly he stopped, frozen in place. He couldn't be sure, but he got the impression that he was now not alone in the darkness. He shifted his weight onto his left leg and rose up to a kneeling position. The feeling stayed with him.

"H-hello? Is anyone there?"

His voice reverberated off the cold walls in the distance. The feeling of being watched began to seep into his body, unnerving him.

"John?"

He waited in silence.

"Not exactly," replied a deep voice that was way too close for comfort.

A bright light suddenly shone in Sammy's face, blinding him. He reacted by putting up his arms to try to block the piercing light. An unseen set of hands wound thick twine around his wrists in an instant, binding them together. Then, the light was suddenly blacked out, and Sammy could feel his own hot breath on his face. Some sort of hood had been placed over his head. His eyes lit up with stars as a boot connected with the side of his head. His arms were yanked forward, making him sprawl out on the ground. Pain shot through his leg and he yelled out. Another kick to the head connected with his ear which began to bleed. The unseen person or people then began dragging Sammy through the darkness by his arms.

18

Pain rocked Sammy's body as he was dragged through the darkness. Or it could be bright light; he didn't know because of the blackening hood over his head, but he couldn't care less about whether he could see or not. He writhed in the grip of the unseen assailant as he tried desperately to balance his right leg on another part of his body. Occasionally he would yell out in pain. Finally he managed to get his left leg underneath the other leg and provide some support and to keep it off the ground.

While the pain subsided some, his body was still jostled around during the trip. He was breathing heavily, mostly due to trying to deal with the intense pain and to try to stay conscious.

"Damn, you a struggler, ain't ya?" asked the deep male voice.

Sammy's arms were given a solid yank, and he attempted to stop squirming. He couldn't even try to loosen the rope around his wrists because they were gripped hard by the assailant. With the pain somewhat reduced, Sammy wondered what to expect when they arrived wherever it was he was being taken. Maybe he was helping Sammy, but that was hard to imagine with the way he treated him. This would probably make it harder for John to find him as well.

Sammy's left hip scraped against what he imagined was a corner as his arms were bent in that direction and then his body straightened out again. If it was this far to get anywhere, Sammy probably wouldn't have made it out.

"Where are...you taking me...to?" asked Sammy as bouts of pain continued to ripple up his leg.

Suddenly the dragging stopped and Sammy flopped to the ground. Soles crunched on the ground and approached him. Then the toe of a boot struck him in the right cheek, driving the inside of his mouth into and over his teeth. Blood began to flow into his mouth from the cuts. His head rang from the fresh strike and combined with the dull throb from his left ear where he had been kicked previously.

"Shaddap!"

The soles crunched away from him, then his arms were roughly picked up and the dragging resumed. Sammy tried in vain to use his tongue to stop the bleeding. He coughed as the blood trickled down his throat, spraying the inside of the shroud. The faint smell of iron began to permeate his nostrils and made him a little nauseous.

They rounded another corner, this time to Sammy's right as his other hip touched the wall. Just as his body straightened out, they stopped and Sammy's arms were dropped to the ground. He listened as footsteps receded from his position. Moments later there was an audible crack, and he began to hear the hum of commercial lights spin up to full strength. The footsteps returned, and once again the dragging resumed. He was pulled towards his right around another corner.

After a short distance, Sammy's arms were dropped again. He could hear the footsteps come back and stop next to him. Then he felt two large hands thrust themselves underneath his body, one under his back and the other just below his butt. Suddenly Sammy felt weightless as he was lifted straight up in the air. He could feel a slight breeze on his arms as he was swung around. He was lowered down onto a hard surface with speed and his head smacked a flat plank. His right leg again lit up with pain at the rough treatment.

What happened next was a blur. Before he realized what happened Sammy's legs were strapped down. The assailant then strapped down his chest. Sammy raised his hands above his head in an attempt to keep those somewhat free. A beefy strong hand grabbed one of his wrists and slammed Sammy's hands down onto his chest forcing most of the air from his lungs. In his momentary state of shock his wrists were untied and his left arm was strapped down. Regaining his senses Sammy tried to take a swing at the mystery person but missed. A thick chuckle greeted his futile attempt.

"Stop wastin' yer energy, prick. Not before I've had my fun."

Sammy tried again to hit something, swinging his free arm around. A fist connected solidly with Sammy's left cheek, adding to the cuts inside his mouth. It got the message across, as Sammy dropped his right arm in surrender. It was quickly strapped down as well, making him immobile.

Sammy felt the table move but with the hood still over his head he couldn't tell in what direction or how far. The movement stopped, then he heard a click and the table tipped down at his feet. Another click and the table snapped into a full vertical position, the straps holding him against the rough wood tightly. The assailant stood in front of him and began checking the straps, tightening them even more which caused him to grunt in pain as his skin was pinched by the thick leather and buckles.

"We don't wantcha fallin' out now, do we."

Satisfied that Sammy wasn't going to escape anytime soon, he finally whipped off the black hood from Sammy's head. The bright light tore into his eyes that had become accustomed to the dark environment, and he squinted against it.

"Well ain't you a handsome one."

Fear and interest helped his eyes to adjust in an instant, and he stared back at a mountain of a man. He easily towered over Sammy's nearly six-foot height, and the stitching in his clothes strained to hold back his muscular bulk. He had stringy dark brown hair that desperately needed a wash. His crooked smile made Sammy feel uneasy to his core.

"What the hell do you want? Let me out of here!"

"Tsk, tsk." A thick finger wagged in disapproval. "Such language from a purdy boy."

Sammy struggled against the leather restraints but they wouldn't give an inch. The large man slowly approached, grin expanding as he watched his prey squirm. Sammy stopped struggling and looked up at a face set with determination, with a goal of control over him. He wasn't about to give him the satisfaction and spat in the brute's face.

The bulging eyes protected themselves with thick eyelids as Sammy's spit trickled down the assailant's face. Seconds ticked by as he waited for some response. He felt his defiance slowly melt to fear as the large man didn't move. Sammy could feel that something was going to happen, and it wouldn't be good.

Like lightning he struck, hitting Sammy in the gut then backhanding him across the face. His finger nails cut lightly into Sammy's nose causing a fresh flow of blood. Slightly hunched over and breathing heavily, the assailant slowly gathered himself and held back from further punishing his victim.

"You lucky, punk boy. The last guy who did that nearly got his face pummeled through the floor of the ring."

"You...wre-...wrestled?" His breath came in gasps as his insides tried to unclench from the surprise shot.

The assailant turned and walked to the far wall. He reached up and took down a long unusual device from the wall.

"Boxed," he replied over his shoulder.

"Me...too."

He swiveled around and faced Sammy, holding the device like a rifle, pointed at him.

"Good. That means ya'll in shape. You'll last longer for more fun."

An audible *Pop!* escaped from the gun-like device.

19

Thwack!

Sammy looked down to see what had struck the wood table. With his body still firmly strapped down, his head had limited range of motion. Then he saw a crimson color slowly work through his white shirt fibers from the left side of his stomach. Shock registered in his brain just before the pain hit. He gritted his teeth and squinted in an attempt to weather the pain storm. A round metal disc with the edge of a razor had sliced through his skin and got embedded in the wood table, creating a gash a few inches long.

"Got ya!" The muscle-bound man grinned his crooked smile and chuckled.

"What the hell are you doing?!" he screamed.

"Jus' havin' a little fun. Good, yeah, wiggle some more."

Sammy watched as he shouldered the razor gun again, taking his time in choosing his next target.

"W-Wait! What do you want? I'm sure I've – Gaahh!"

A second razor disc made its mark on his arm. Fresh blood trickled down the wood table. He strained against the straps as he struggled to deal with the biting pain. A third disc sliced through his inner thigh, narrowly missing the femoral artery. He yelled out in pain and threw a few cuss words towards his assailant.

"Spread yer hand out."

"What?"

"I said spread yer hand out, dammit!" He trained the disc gun on Sammy's face. "Or do ya wanna try to catch one with yer teeth?"

Sammy splayed his fingers out on both hands against the cold wood, unsure which hand was going to get cut up. He silently said a prayer that the disc would miss its mark. Surprised with himself, Sammy watched him pick his spot on his left hand.

Pop!

At the sound of the air pushing the sharp disc towards his hand, Sammy squinted at the coming pain.

Thwack!

For a few seconds, he waited for the pain to hit. With nothing noticeable having happened to his hand, he tilted his head down. Unbelievably, the disc had missed his middle and fore fingers and was buried half-way into the wood between them. He exhaled loudly and closed his eyes, thankful for his luck.

"You a lucky bastard."

Sammy opened his eyes and looked at the large man. He could see anger in his face from across the room.

"I hate that."

Trying to hold the disc gun steady, the large man again tried to hit one of Sammy's fingers. He narrowly missed his left pinky finger.

"Sonofabitch! Are you shitting me?" he yelled at no one in particular. He was breathing heavy now, filling with rage. Like a little kid throwing a tantrum in a store, he stomped his feet in disgust. Then he swung the gun up at Sammy again and pulled the trigger in rapid succession.

In short order, Sammy's clothes were soaked from his blood. The discs had connected with his right wrist, an ankle, cut through the top of his hair, and one pierced his thigh dead-on; this one sank deep to the bone. A few others nicked Sammy in a few other places. The table looked like the end of a knife throwing act with all of the little metal discs sticking out, though one that had gone terribly wrong; blood began to pool on the floor beneath him.

The assailant's rage hadn't been satiated, as he pulled the trigger a few more times with no corresponding discs flying away. He threw down the disc gun in a huff and looked around the room wildly. He found his next choice of weapon in a bull whip hanging high up on the wall behind him. He pulled it down and uncoiled it. Sammy caught a glimmer of joy in his eyes as he warmed up with a quick snap of the whip.

The next few minutes were a blur of pain. He was worked over with the bull whip, some snaps occurring just a fraction of an inch from his face. Many times the assailant connected with one of the wounds from the metal discs, and each time Sammy would yelp in pain and squirm what little he could in an act of protection and preservation. He connected with Sammy's face just above the eye, causing a large welt to form, and the rest of his body slowly turned black and blue as the end of the whip harshly kissed various parts of his body.

Still flinching, Sammy realized that the assailant had stopped whipping him. He opened his good eye to see him replace the whip on the wall, pick up the disc gun and disappear out the door. Waves of relief overcame Sammy, and he passed out, welcoming the darkness.

20

John's headlamp beam cut like a knife through the thick darkness. He was barely five feet into the mine entrance and already it felt like he was drowning in the dark. Pulling out his GPS unit, he realized it would be impossible to get satellite signals underground, and turned it off. He replaced it in his waist pack and instead pulled out an old-fashioned compass. Unless there was an abundance of magnetic material in the mine, his compass should still work underground and point to magnetic North. He watched as the needle slowly turned in its liquid housing, the red half of the needle settling on the northerly direction.

The mine was hand-carved with picks and shovels. Old timbers were supporting the rock around him and keeping it from collapsing under its own weight. A thick cross-beam was supported on either end with square vertical timbers, and angled pieces helped reinforce the corners. The supports were spaced about eighteen inches apart, and they stretched into the blackness. For a few moments, he could imagine the hard, back-breaking work that would have had to happen just to make the mine another twelve inches deeper into the earth.

As he progressed further into the mine, John realized that he should start mapping his progress so he could more easily find his way out once he found Sammy. He located a small carpenters pencil and a clean, folded sheet of paper in his waist pack. Carefully he marked the mine entrance and direction on the paper, including the compass direction of North. Satisfied with his efforts, he again pushed forward through the darkness. Occasionally he would stop to add to his map.

The mine passage began to wind back and forth, as the original miners had tried to increase their success in following the mineral vein they sought. He came to a cross passage, unsure which direction to follow. Suddenly getting an idea, he pulled out the compass. Since he recalled the compass direction he took to get to the mine, it made sense that he should try to double back in the opposite direction in order to get to Sammy. The compass settled into position, and he had his answer. He turned left and continued deeper into the mine.

The passage was straight for nearly a hundred feet or so, then began to curve toward the right. As he continued to follow the passage, he was sure that he would end up back at the intersection where he turned left. After nearly twenty minutes, he was vindicated as he arrived at the intersection. Knowing that going right would just lead him back around the same passage, he instead turned left to explore this new passage.

Stopping every so often to continue to build his map was slowing down John's progress, but he would need it if he was ever to get out of the mine alive. He only hoped that he could get to his friend before anything else bad happened to him. If he was losing blood, he could go into shock, even die. No, he needed to continue mapping the mine so that he could expedite their exit once he finally found Sammy and get him to medical help.

This passage also continued straight away from the intersection, then began to curve to the right. He continued to map, checking his compass occasionally to make sure that he was getting the directions as accurate as possible. When he started down this passageway, he was going due East, but after having come around a large curve he was now facing due West. By his calculations, if he continued straight West, he would eventually run into the initial passage he took as he entered the mine. He didn't recall seeing any side passages on his way into the mine, nor did he see any doors that might indicate a room or other passages.

As he continued down the passage, he passed the point where he figured he should have crossed paths with the main entrance passage. He continued on at least another fifty feet, and the passage opened up into a room that was hewn out of the rock by the miners. It was a rough rectangle in size, about eight feet wide and twelve feet long. Thick, old timbers were positioned throughout the room to give support to the ceiling and prevent it from falling in. Despite all of the support, there were small piles of dirt and rock in a few places in the room, giving evidence that even as good as the miner's efforts were, nothing lasted forever without upkeep.

Hanging on one of the timbers near the center of the room was an old kerosene lantern. Amazingly, the glass globe was still intact after all of these years. Out of curiosity, he shook the lantern a little, and could hear liquid sloshing around in the bottom fuel chamber. He was a little unnerved by this discovery, as it meant that someone had been here recently and had used or at least filled this lantern.

His anxiety level went up a few notches and for a moment he felt as though he was being watched. He spun in a circle, his headlamp beam revealing rock and wood all around him, but no one else was with him. Satisfied for the moment but still on edge, he dug into his waist pack and extracted a small lighter. Flicking it on, he managed to light the lantern, which eased his anxiety a bit.

He took out the map he had been making and looked at it in the additional light. Obviously he had been heading down into the Earth as he was going along the passageways. It had been so subtle that he hadn't noticed it at the time, plus he had been preoccupied with making the map. He figured that he had descended at least 20 feet and possibly more with all of the distance that he had covered.

As he put away his map, he looked around the rock room again. This time he noticed that there was a passageway exiting the room on the far side from where he entered. He needed to forge ahead, so he went back to the lantern to blow it out. Just as he was about to extinguish the light, he stopped himself. He should leave the lantern on in case he took other passageways that led him back here. He shook the lantern again, heard the fuel slosh around the tank, and guessed that there was at least two hours worth of kerosene. Hopefully it would help him decipher where some of the passageways went.

To make it easier to see the light from further down the passageway, he moved the lamp to the ground just at the entrance. He set off down the carved out passage, which quickly turned to the right. After going a little more than fifty feet, John found himself again at a crossroads in the mine. He updated his map, then looked behind him. He could see the soft light from the lantern back in the room penetrate to the crossroads. If he came back around to this same intersection, he should be able to verify it with the lantern light.

He elected to continue straight through the intersection. This passage continued straight, then began to curve around to the right. Following and mapping, he ended up at another crossroads. To verify that he wasn't at the previous intersection, he briefly doused his headlamp and was plunged into a nearly suffocating darkness and silence. Seeing no light from anywhere, he quickly turned on his headlamp and consulted his map. It appeared that from this intersection he should be able to go right and meet back up with the previous intersection, and should be able to verify this with the light from the lantern. He moved out to his right, and was shortly back where he thought he would end up. He looked to his left, down the passageway that led to the large room, expecting to see some faint light from the lantern.

Of course, his headlamp probably drowned out any light from the lantern as he looked down the passage, so he again turned off his headlamp. He stared into the blackness, but could see no light. Confused, he turned his headlamp back on and again consulted his map. He should be back at the intersection he encountered just after he left the lantern room. But obviously he wasn't, or else he would have seen the light coming down the hallway.

To satisfy his curiosity, he took a left and went towards the lantern room. The passageway seemed to be how he remembered it, but he was going in reverse from when he first went through this passageway, so he wasn't sure if it was curving enough to the left to be the same passageway. Then he was in the room again, only the lantern wasn't on the ground where he left it. He went to the nail on the central timber where he first found the lantern, and it too was bare. Just what the heck was going on?

21

Everything looked right, felt right, except for the missing lantern. He was in the same room, that John was sure of, but what had happened to the lantern? He took a moment to think about the possibilities. One, he could actually be in a different room. He was sure that this was highly unlikely, but since this was the first time he had ever been in this mine, or any mine for that matter, it was still a possibility.

Another possibility was that an animal had made off with the lantern. A dog? It would have had to have been a larger animal that could have picked up the lantern and carried it off, probably by grasping the handle in its mouth. Maybe a wolf or coyote could have done it. But regardless of the animal, what would it have been doing this deep in the mine? And where would it have taken it?

No, John couldn't believe that an animal would have taken the lantern. If an animal didn't take it, and he was sure that he was in the right room, then it left one possibility that sent shivers up and down his spine. With the lantern gone, it would mean that there was another person in the mine with him.

But why take the lantern and then disappear? Why not attempt to communicate and find out who else was in the mine? But of course, it became plainly obvious to him at that moment. The same person who was behind the voice in the church was probably also behind the lantern disappearing. He suddenly got the feeling that he was being watched again, and spun around to look around the room. It was empty.

Alone, trying to find his friend, he elected to press forward once again. He said a short prayer under his breath as he again left the room and got to the intersection. He turned right and went back to the other intersection, retracing his steps from just a little while earlier. He got to the other intersection, but now it was a T; he could go forward or take a left and go back around the large loop. There was no passageway to his right. Confused, he again withdrew his crude map and confirmed that when he passed through this intersection previously there was a passage leading off to his right. Now, it was gone.

If his map was indeed wrong, he should try to confirm that before pressing on and making even more mistakes. He chose to take a left and go around what should be a large loop that ended back at the first intersection just beyond the lantern room. Sure enough, he came back to this intersection, and he felt a little better about his mapping abilities. He must have thought there was a passageway there and marked it as such on his map.

Satisfied, he took a left towards what should now be the T in the passageways. He moved confidently down the passage, not worrying about mapping any of the tunnel as he had already been here numerous times. After ten minutes of walking, he had a suspicion that he had gone further than what he should have. He went a little bit more, then stopped. He should have hit the T by now, but all that he saw was a straight passage leading into darkness in both directions.

He doubled back, wanting to get back to the intersection that led to the lantern room. He ended at another T intersection, this time with passages to his left and right. It was about the same amount of time to walk back, so he guessed that going left would take him to the lantern room, and it did.

Not wanting to stay in the area, he made his way across the lantern room to the other exit to start making his way back to other intersections to give them a try. Only, the other exit wasn't there. The only way out of this room was to go out the way he came in.

"All right, what the heck is going on?"

He half expected an answer from the same voice from the church. Silence greeted him instead. He stood in the middle of the room, looking back and forth between the passage he came in from and the place on the rock wall where the other way out used to be. Finally he decided to leave the room again, not sure what he should be expecting at the intersection. If it was even there anymore.

Surprisingly, the intersection was the same as it was when he last passed through it. He had come from the right, but he was tempted to go straight ahead. He had abandoned any hope at this point of continuing to update his map, since every time he thought he had things mapped correctly he encountered something that wasn't the same as he had recorded it before.

He turned right and made his way down the now-familiar passageway. A little ways down the passage made an abrupt left turn. He continued to follow the passage around a gentle curve, and after an additional half-hour's walking he ended back up at the lantern room, or at least a room that looked nearly identical to the last one he was in.

Frustrated, tired and cold, he sat down and leaned against one of the timbers along the wall. He couldn't get back out the way he originally came in, and now something was happening with the mine passageways that they were changing on him. He didn't know how, but he was sure that it had a connection to what happened with Sammy and the voice.

He switched off his headlamp to conserve whatever power was left in the batteries. Absently, he rummaged through his waist pack in the dark, searching for a beef jerky stick that he had put there before they left that morning. He contemplated his next move as he bit a piece of jerky from the stick.

One thing that he was sure of was that he was in just as bad a position as Sammy was. He wasn't certain if he would be able to rescue his friend, let alone get himself out of this mess. He might as well pick a passage direction and stick with it, rather than try to figure out the ever-changing passages that he'd been subjected to thus far.

He popped the remaining piece of jerky into his mouth. Something caught the corner of his eye, and he turned to the single exit from the room. A dull splash of light filled the passageway entrance and began to grow stronger.

22

Sammy couldn't tell if he was awake or not. Or perhaps dead. Everything was black and the only thing he could hear was his own breathing. He tried to move his arm, but it held firm. He tried twisting it, and that's when the soreness registered. It radiated from his right arm into his chest and then burst out to the rest of his body. He winced from the intensity, then groaned as the act of wincing caused further pain from the welt above his left eye.

"Son of a bitch."

Even speaking hurt. He tried moving his legs, having forgotten the earlier descent he took from the church.

"Aaahh! Dammit!"

Lightning shot from his leg through the rest of his body, and he went limp against restraints as he fought to retain consciousness. Minutes passed until he was ready to try anything again. This time he started small, trying to open his eyes and take stock of his situation. His right eye opened okay, and things slowly came into focus. His left eye remained shut, and he recalled with anger the whip strike that caused the inflammation that now caused his cyclops vision.

The light in the room was off, but the door was left open and light from the hallway gave enough illumination for him to see. Using his good eye, he slowly looked over his body. He had been cut numerous times and blood had soaked through his clothes and dripped onto the floor. It appeared that most of the cuts had at least scabbed over and had stopped bleeding. He could also see his skin was mottled with black and blue welts from the whip strikes.

"Now, how the hell am I gonna get outta here?"

Sammy was not looking forward to having another encounter with the large assailant, especially if he was still strapped to the table. He started looking around for something that could get him out of the straps, then realized that it wouldn't do any good if he couldn't reach whatever it was he might find. Somehow, he would have to maneuver himself out of the restraints.

He looked at all of the restraints and how they held him in. They were like belt buckles – simple to operate but also very effective at holding whatever it was they were secured against. The only ones that really mattered were the ones holding his arms; once he got one of his arms free he should be able to undo the rest of the buckles and get himself out.

He first tried his right arm which had mostly escaped punishment except for the occasional whipping. None of the metal discs had struck his right arm, so he was hoping he might be able to muscle his way out of the restraint, or at least have the range of motion to wriggle it out. Unfortunately, no amount of twisting, yanking or pulling managed to make a difference.

Frustrated, he turned to his left arm. It had been struck by a metal disc, and the evidence showed on the brown table that was streaked to the floor with dull crimson. He gingerly tried twisting his left arm, not wanting to experience any shocks of pain. He was rewarded with only dull throbbing as blood worked through the damaged tissue and began to repair it. In the midst of his efforts, he noticed that the restraint on this arm was noticeably looser than on his right arm. He tried to manipulate his arm a little more forcefully in an attempt to determine just how loose it was. That was when he noticed it.

As he flexed out his left arm, he noticed that the restraint had a cut in it. In fact, it was cut nearly half-way through. It must have happened when his arm was cut with the metal disc; the disc hit part of the restraint and went deep enough to cut into his arm. He put a little pressure on the restraint and felt it give. This was his only chance at escape...and survival.

23

John rubbed his eyes in disbelief. That really was light coming from the passageway. And it was getting closer. Light began to spill from the passageway into the room. He could hear the footsteps approaching as the sound echoed off of the rock walls. Questions swirled in his mind: Where did this person come from? How did he not see him before? Was he the one who took the lantern?

As the light continued to get brighter, the timbers holding up the ceiling cast shadows that resembled prison bars. John felt like the prisoner with the warden coming to check on the inmates. He left his headlamp off, not wanting to draw attention to his presence just yet.

And then the lantern appeared at the passageway entrance. It was much brighter than the kerosene lamp John had found in the room. He tried to see who was behind the light, but its intensity blinded him from seeing beyond. He could only see the edges of fingers curled around the handle of the lantern, causing it to seem otherworldly, floating in air. The lantern held its position, unmoving.

"H-hello?" John asked, breaking the silence.

The lantern remained motionless, like a sentry. John stood up but stayed where he was. He called out again. This time a second hand appeared in the light. It beckoned him to come forward.

"Need help finding your way out?" a deep voice asked.

John made his way around the timbers toward the voice and lantern. As he got closer, he threw his hand up in front of him, shielding the main point of light from view. This allowed him to see that there was, in fact, someone behind the lantern. A very big someone. It looked like he took up nearly the whole space of the passageway.

John got up to the lantern, which was held at nearly the level of his face. He could see just how large the hand was holding the lamp. His eyes traveled over the immense body looming over him. There were muscles over muscles, and he could make out the telltale veins that indicated someone who lifted weights, heavy weights, regularly. He made his way up to the stoic face. Large, penetrating eyes stared back at him from a chiseled but unremarkable face.

"Can you help me get out?" John asked.

The answer took a little too long for John's comfort.

"Sure can...purdy boy."

A grin slowly started to appear on the large man's face.

24

With the pressure and twisting he did with his left arm, the light scab over the cut gave way and fresh blood started flowing down the table again. Sammy stretched out his arm as far as it would go to move the restraint further up his forearm. He quickly looked back toward the doorway and listened for any sound that might indicate that the large man was coming back.

Adrenaline had flooded his body and he was nearly jumping in the restraints. For a full minute he strained to hear anything from the hallway. Satisfied that he wouldn't be surprised, he turned again to his left arm and the half-cut restraint. He knew that it would be painful, but this was his only shot at getting out. He took a deep breath, then began applying pressure to the restraint on his arm.

Not much happened. He could feel the soreness throughout his arm and his body as his muscles tried to respond to his request. Blood continued to drip from his arm, which was now straining against the leather. He gritted his teeth and redoubled his efforts. The rest of his body, in an attempt to gain leverage against the table, was also putting stress on the other restraints.

The skin on his arm around the restraint was starting to turn white from the pressure that was cutting off blood circulation. He started grunting and putting as much of his whole body into the effort of breaking through the restraint as he could. Then he felt something give.

He stopped and his eyes opened wide with fear – fear that he had torn something in his arm. He quickly looked over at his arm and everything looked okay. He wriggled his fingers to be sure that they were still all in working order. No new pain and he exhaled with relief. He looked back again at the restraint but didn't notice anything different with it.

"Damn."

Maybe it was one of the other restraints that had loosened a bit. Nice, but he doubted that one of them would just suddenly pop open for him. He started to readjust his arm again, then stopped. He slowly pressed his arm against the restraint again, and that's when he saw the little bit of jagged edges at the bottom of the cut in the restraint. He had actually started to break through!

He immediately set to work again on the restraint. He knew that his time was only getting shorter and that the large man could be back anytime. He gritted his teeth and threw all that he had at the restraint. Blood once again flowed from his arm, and he felt the edges of the leather start to bite into his flesh. He jerked his body back and forth to try to put even more pressure onto the restraint.

He heard a snap, and then his left arm was swinging free. It crossed his chest and smacked into his right arm. It took him a few moments to register that he'd managed to do it, to break through the restraint. With the physical abuse he'd taken at the hands of the assailant and loss of blood from the cuts, he felt spent and just hung against the rest of the restrains trying to gather up his strength again.

After a few minutes, he began working at the other buckles with his free hand. Having only one hand to work the restraints proved taxing and it took a while to release the first one that was around his chest. The others came quicker, and he soon found himself crumpled on the floor in a mix of pain and relief. Using the leather restraints he pulled himself up onto his good leg and again rested against the table. He was weak, and he knew that he needed both medical treatment and food, quickly.

He hobbled to the doorway, then stopped and listened again for any sounds. Hearing nothing, he continued out into the brightly lit hallway. Like a drunk coming out of a bar at closing time, Sammy staggered down the hallway, bouncing off the walls like a pinball. Nearly every hop he made his other leg would send off shots of pain as it hit the floor. Stumbling forward, his shoulder smacked hard against a large stone in the wall. He winced in pain from both his leg and his left shoulder, and he rested against the wall, breathing heavily.

In front of him, part of the wall pivoted inward as a new entryway opened up. He must have made enough noise to get the attention of his captor. He waited to see the hulking man emerge from the new opening, and he closed his eyes, bracing himself for the physical onslaught he knew would be coming.

Nothing. No hands grabbed him roughly, no yelling or physical abuse. He opened his eyes to the harsh fluorescent light, and the hallway was empty. He pushed himself away from the wall and hobbled over to the new opening. Looking through the doorway, Sammy was shocked at what he saw.

25

John gave the large man a blank stare, trying to figure out exactly what he meant or why he was smiling. The grin transformed into a full-on smile with yellowing teeth. That was the last image John had in his eyes.

With cat-like reflexes, the large man swept the headlamp from John's head, dropping it on the ground. His other hand dropped the lantern on the ground, and the light went out, enveloping them in the dark. The large man struck John in the solar plexus, doubling him over. He then swept John's feet out from under him, and John dropped hard to the ground.

John's hands and feet were bound and a cloth bag was roughly slid over his head. The punch to his chest left John struggling for breath and unable to fight back. The large man yanked on John's arms, then began dragging him through the darkness. They turned left and John's torso and legs scraped along the rough rock and dirt wall.

"Wha-what are you doing? Where are you taking me?"

The large man stopped and dropped John's hands on the ground. He walked back and kicked John in the stomach, hard. John curled up like a caterpillar protecting itself and moaned.

"No talkin', purdy boy."

He picked up John's hands and continued dragging down the mine passageways. The pain in John's gut slowly subsided as they made their way, taking first a right then a left. John had tried to make a mental map of the turns they were making, but he could only guess at how far apart each of them were, and that wasn't taking into account that if he were able to see where they were going that there weren't other turnoffs that they were not taking.

He dared not ask any more questions until after they had stopped, though he had plenty of them. He wondered if the brute had also found Sammy, and what he might have done to him if he had. Sammy was already in rough shape from the fall through the church floor, he didn't need anyone beating him to a pulp.

John felt his hands released and they dropped to the ground. The back of his left hand struck a sharp rock and sent a jolt of pain up his arm.

"Ungh! Gee thanks."

A few footsteps, then John could feel the large man's boot pressing on his hands, driving the sharp stone further into his hand.

"AH! Damn, stop it, STOP IT!"

"Yous gonna be quiet then?"

"Y-yes! I'll be quiet."

The boot came off his hands, then struck John on his head. The hard sole caused a gash that immediately started bleeding, matting his hair under the hood.

"That's not bein' quiet, boy! Now, are you gonna shut up?"

John struggled to be as silent as he could be, praying that it would be enough and he would leave him alone. After a few moments, the large man went back to what he was doing, and John exhaled in relief. Not only did his clothes get torn on the trip, but now his hand and head were bleeding and throbbing.

The large man returned and lifted John up by his arm pits. He dragged John backwards a few feet then roughly set him in a hard, cold, wooden chair. The man put a leather belt around his chest and cinched it down tightly. He did the same with each of John's legs, securing them to the legs of the chair.

"Hold yer hands above yer head."

Meekly, John did as he was instructed. He felt the edge of a board press up against his chest. He looked like a kid who needed to be called on so badly that he was using both hands to try to get the teacher's attention. The man grabbed his hands and slammed them onto the hard wooden table. He unbound John's wrists, then started to secure his left hand to the table with a leather strap.

Sensing an opportunity, John used his free hand to try undo the restraint across his chest. He frantically felt around for a strap or a buckle that he could undo. The man looked back and smirked.

"You ain't gettin' outta the chair, son. Release is in the back. Good luck reachin' it."

John stopped his fruitless search, anger and fear welling up inside him. When the man went back to his other hand, John tried to punch him. He succeeded in making contact with his ear. To John's surprise, the man stopped what he was doing and howled in pain.

"Gah! Little bastard, you just got the sentence!"

Blood started to run from his right ear, which infuriated him. He let out a loud yell then unloaded on John with his fists. A dozen strikes landed on John's face and arms as he tried in vain to defend against the unseen attacker. His nose was broken and bloodied, his jaw was sore and had lost a tooth, and multiple fingers had been jammed from the force of the man's fists as he tried in vain to protect himself.

The man slunk a few feet away and attempted to gather himself together. He was still breathing hard and fought against the urge to simply finish off John with his fists. His breaths started to turn into stilted laughs, which turned into wild laughter as he envisioned the fun soon to come. He returned to where John was strapped to the chair and quickly finished strapping down his arms to the table. He ripped off the cloth sack from John's head.

"Ready for the fun, prick?"

26

Sammy had never seen so much computer and video equipment in one place before. He imagined that a television control studio would look something like this room. On the wall opposite the doorway was a full-width desk with numerous keyboards, small joysticks and mice, and papers scattered over the rest of the open space. Above the desk the rest of the wall was covered with a grid of flat panel computer screens. Some of the larger screens were split into four quadrants, each quadrant showing a different image. These were down lower to the desk top. Higher screens near the ceiling showed full size images. Underneath the desk, on each end, were multiple computer towers.

On his left was a large map that covered nearly the entire wall. The door was covering up some of the map, but he could immediately tell that it was of their current area, and that it was a very sophisticated map. It showed contour lines, latitude and longitude markings, and other standard map markings. It had been improved with hand markings, presumably by the large man, that marked numerous spots around the entire forest.

Across from the map was another smaller table, this one holding various pieces of outdoor gear: binoculars, GPS units, steel water bottles, carabiners and other assorted odds and ends. On the same wall as the doorway was a tall green metal cabinet. It looked to be army surplus, sporting scratched green paint all over and a large white circle in the middle of the doors with a red plus sign indicating it once held medical supplies.

Sammy sat in the office chair at the large monitor bank and looked at what was showing on the different screens. The screens that were divided up into quadrants showed images from out in the forest. As he scanned them, he saw that one was showing his and John's campsite. As if answering his unuttered question, he watched a large crow swoop down and land on the ground close to where they'd had a roaring fire going just the evening before.

"Son of a bitch was spying on us!"

As he scrutinized more of the video images, he could identify some of them as the locations where they had found the various geocaches that had led them to the church. He looked up at the upper bank of monitors, and noticed that one of them showed a wide-angle shot of the interior of the little church.

Sammy leaned back in the chair and ran his hands through his short black hair as he realized the scope of what was going on. He got up on his good leg and hopped over to the map wall. He quickly found the main highway that had led them to the small town of Drummond. From there, he traced the narrow forest road to where they turned off on a logging trail. He followed that to where their camping spot was. Right at that spot was a black star made by a Sharpie.

He turned back towards the bank of monitors. Yup, there was the live video feed from their camp. Returning to the map, he slowly moved his finger in the direction they went for the first geocache. There was another black star at that spot, as there was for the other caches that they had found.

He had watched them move from cache to cache through the forest until they made it to the small church. He had watched as they explored the church, and had just been waiting for one of them to step behind the pulpit in the front. Sammy had been the unlucky one to do so. Now, John was out looking for a way to get to him.

"Oh, shit."

What had John said just before he left the church? That he needed to go to another set of coordinates. For sure it was his assailant that had given John those coordinates. But where would he go? He scoured the wall map for anything around the church. He didn't see any Sharpie markings like he did for the cameras. And it couldn't be too far away from the church, otherwise it would be difficult to deal with everything he had already set up here.

As part of the normal markings that were on the map, there were indications of various structures, both natural and man-made. There were railroad lines, electric transmission lines, waterfalls, communications towers, old abandoned mines... That was it. There was an abandoned mine only a few hundred yards from the church marked on the map.

He turned back to the bank of monitors. There it was, on one of the divided screens, a shot of the entrance to a mine. He could see a few boards scattered over the ground near the entrance. That had to be it.

He could only imagine what might be waiting for John once he had gotten into the mine. Tunnels could be flooded, they could collapse, there could be poisonous gases, or any number of other things, not to mention what the large man might do. That had to be why he had left Sammy to bleed to death strapped to the table.

Suddenly he had a thought. With all of the cameras that he had rigged up, maybe he had a few up in the mine where he could see where John was. He quickly began to look again at all of the screens. None of the quad monitors held anything but outdoor shots and the church. He looked at the larger monitors above those, and found a camera shot of the torture room he had previously been in. He was shocked at how much blood was on the table face and the floor.

The next screen he saw made him look twice. It was pretty dark owing to only a single dim light source. He hopped closer to get a better look. He continued to stare at it, not understanding what he was looking at. Then something on the screen moved.

"Oh my God!"

27

In the dim light it took a little time for John's eyes to adjust and refocus. The light was partially blocked by the hulking man standing in front of him. John could see that he had stringy straight hair, a thick neck supporting a large, somewhat lumpy head. Broad shoulders held up meaty arms and rested atop his muscled torso. He couldn't be quite sure, but he thought he saw a crooked smile on his face.

"Who are you and what do you want with me?"

For a moment the imposing man thought about how he should answer the questions, if he desired to. John took the time to test the restraints and found them to offer barely any give.

"Let's keep me anonymous for the time being, eh? You jus call me Woodsman. And I want to have some fun."

"What did you do with my friend?"

The Woodsman chuckled. "He made a fun target."

John stared back at him, hatred brewing inside him. He again struggled against the restraints, hoping to loosen them just a little.

"What did you do to him?" John yelled.

The Woodsman turned away and walked to a far corner of the carved out room. John's eyes followed him as he walked away, then noticed that this room was very similar to the lantern room with one key difference: there were no supporting timbers in this room. Instead, a steel frame lined the ceiling and transferred the weight to a half-dozen concrete columns around the perimeter of the room. It made the room seem twice as big even though it was no bigger than the other one.

"I said, what did you do to him?" John yelled again.

"That's it," the Woodsman grumbled under his breath, "just get me going. You'll be even more sorry than you already are."

John could hear the Woodsman murmuring to himself, and it infuriated him even more. He struggled harder against the restraints, rocking himself from side to side. The Woodsman grabbed something and returned to his struggling prey.

"I got a special treat for ya." The Woodsman held up a dingy hacksaw and grinned down at John.

John stopped working against the restraints and looked up to see a face filled with anticipation. His heartbeat thundered in his ears and he swallowed hard.

"W-w-what are you going to do?"

"You get to play a little game. You see how long you remain conscious."

John didn't know what sort of things were involved with this game but he was sure he wouldn't like any of it. The hacksaw didn't inspire any confidence either. The Woodsman lumbered around behind John and stood to his right side.

"Let's start to play."

Eagerly the Woodsman lunged forward with his left hand and grasped John's right hand. His large hand engulfed John's and manipulated his fingers so that John's pinky was splayed out on the table with the others held firm. John struggled in vain to burrow his pinky inside of the large hand for protection, and strained against the wrist strap on the table.

"What the hell are you doing?" screamed John.

The Woodsman released John's hand, only to slam his elbow into John's face. His head snapped back, and the pain of a broken nose hit. Blood began flowing down his face. The Woodsman returned his iron grip to John's hand, exposing his pinky once again. He brought up the hacksaw with his right hand and set it against John's little finger.

John's life went into slow-motion. He could hear himself screaming and the Woodsman laughing as he drew the hacksaw back, slicing into the meat of his finger. His adrenaline was firing hard, which helped to dull the intense sharp pains registering in his brain. The chair was jumping off the ground with John's efforts to somehow, some way escape the torture being inflicted on him.

As the Woodsman pushed the blade forward, John could both hear and feel it strike bone. It sounded like sawing through a thick PVC pipe. John couldn't stop screaming from the horror of the situation. He desperately wanted to look away, but was also afraid to.

"Damn you a loud one!"

To John's shock and disbelief, the Woodsman started to saw faster. Blood from his finger spurted over the table and covered the hacksaw blade. The Woodsman looked like a deranged butcher, frantically sawing away with a lusty look on his face. John continued to writhe in pain and scream as the Woodsman finished cutting through his finger.

When the final cut sliced through the last ribbon of flesh, the Woodsman stood there, bent over the table, his body relaxing. He looked calm, serene and satisfied, like he had just had an orgasm. He blocked out John's screaming and thrashing, which confused and frightened John even more.

"W-w-what the hell?! You just cut off my f-f-finger! Oh my God. I'm going to bleed to death down here. Help. Help! Somebody help!"

With John yelling for help it snapped the Woodsman out of his daze. He yanked his head around and stared at his noisy companion. He swung his left hand back and connected with John's already broken nose, smashing it into his skull. Blinding white pain seared through John's head, shocking him so much that he couldn't take a breath for a few seconds. Blood continued rolling down his face, and he looked like he had been in a street brawl. His finger continued to bleed onto the table, the cut off tip resting mere inches from the rest of his body.

The Woodsman slowly stood back up and walked back over to the far side of the room where he had gotten the hacksaw. He dropped the saw on the ground, then pulled off the heavy cloth that had been covering a hand truck. Moving the cart like it was a toy, he pulled it over in front of John. Dumbfounded, John watched as the Woodsman attached two alligator clips to the posts on a battery. The battery was wired in series to two other batteries, all of which were mounted on shelves that had been crudely welded onto the hand truck.

Once again the Woodsman returned to the other side of the room and carried back two large pails filled with water. John had calmed down a little and was taking in everything that the Woodsman was doing. He glanced back down at his right hand and flexed his fingers wide open; he could see a small spot of white bone where his finger had been separated. Seeing it made John nearly faint. The Woodsman slapped his face a little to bring him back.

"Come on, purdy boy, stay with me. The game isn't over yet. But yer surprisin' me. I woulda figured you'd be out before I got done with the little finger."

"Guess I'm toughern you thought." The loss of blood, adrenaline and pure excitement were beginning to take their toll on

John as he began to sound and act like someone who was getting a good buzz from having too many beers.

The Woodsman ignored him and dipped a cup into one of the pails, filling it with water. He walked around behind John and then doused his arm with the cold water.

"What the heck are you doing now?!"

He walked back around the hand truck, dropping the cup back into the pail. Ignoring the question, he produced two metal sticks with sponges on the ends that were connected by wires to the battery set. He dipped the sponges into the water pails, then set them on the table. On the hand truck, he flipped a switch and rotated a dial, then picked the sticks back up.

"Time for the game to continue."

The Woodsman shoved the two sponge sticks onto John's arm. A shot of electricity coursed through his arm and caused it to spasm. It surprised John and his whole body shook involuntarily. Not wanting jumpy game players, the Woodsman punched John in the chest, causing him to cough and gasp for air.

He quickly dipped the sponges in the water again then hit John's other arm, causing it to spasm as well. The shocking only added to his pain, and he struggled in vain against the straps holding him down. The Woodsman removed the sponges and John was breathing heavily, trying to cope with the pain. The Woodsman took the sponges off of the sticks, revealing wet copper prongs. He clicked them together, causing sparks to crackle.

"If you make it through this...well, we'll see."

Moving closer to John's right hand, he positioned the copper prongs inches away from the severed finger. He looked at John's bloody, beaten face, and grinned. The prongs were shoved into the meat of what was left of his finger. The current flowed throughout John's entire body, and he flopped against the restraints like a fish. After nearly a minute, the Woodsman removed the prongs, and John's body went limp.

"Damn, and he was doing so good."

28

The camera position was to the Woodsman's back, and he wasn't moving for a little bit, so all that Sammy could see on the screen was the dull light coming from off camera. Then the hulking brute moved out of the way, and that's when Sammy saw a sight he never imagined in his worst nightmares.

He saw his friend strapped to a chair, seated at a table. His head was slumped forward, but he could see a large red stain on his shirt: blood. His arms were stretched out and strapped down onto the table. His right hand was covered in blood and there was a dark red pool on the table with rivulets streaming away across the table. The Woodsman disappeared off screen, pulling a hand truck behind him.

"Oh my God!" Sammy gasped. "What the hell did he do to you?"

All that he could do was fall against the back of the chair and stare up at the haunting image of his friend, beaten and bloody. Possibly dead. Probably dead. He shook his head in disbelief, thoughts of remorse seeping into his brain.

If only he hadn't pushed them on to the next cache, and then the next one, they would probably be back at camp, enjoying a s'more and a cold beer. They'd be cracking jokes and making plans for their next excursion. Now they were trying to escape from a sick brute bent on torture. He continued looking at the limp body of his friend, and his sorrow quickly turned to anger.

He began to look around the room for something to defend himself with. Unfortunately, aside from the few items on the side table, everything else was bolted down. He struggled up from the chair and hobbled over to the old green cabinet and ripped open the doors. He rifled through the shelves in the cabinet, spilling odds and ends onto the floor but finding nothing worthy of a weapon.

"Damn!"

He slammed the cabinet doors shut. For the second time, he scanned the room for anything that might be able to be used as a weapon. His anger at the situation he helped to create for himself and his friend was compounded by the frustration in not finding something quickly to use as a weapon. He slammed his hand down onto the side table and the small items jumped in response.

He hobbled back over by the chair and again took in all of the different cameras that were strewn about the forest. His anger rose into rage, and he grasped the office chair and raised it up, readying to throw it against monitors.

"Ah wouldn't do that, sonny."

Sammy whipped his head around to find the Woodsman standing in the doorway. He filled nearly the entire space and didn't look very pleased that Sammy had managed to free himself.

"Think a second time before you do somethin' that you'll regret."

Seeing his torturer only added fuel to the rage burning inside him. He slowly turned to face the monster, but didn't put the chair down.

"What did you do to him?" Sammy asked through gritted teeth.

"Your friend? Oh, he had fun playing a game. But a little tuckered out now."

"Is he dead?"

"Hope not, he's still got nine fingers left."

The Woodsman grinned from ear to ear, obviously proud with what he had done. Sammy, unable to imagine just what he did to John to cause a comment such as what was just uttered, let his rage boil over. He whipped the office chair at the bulk in the doorway as hard as he was able to with only one leg firmly planted for leverage. The Woodsman threw up his arm in defense, but one of the hard plastic wheels on the base managed to poke itself into his eye. He yelled out and covered his eye, bending over in reflex to provide his face with further protection.

The chair bounced on the floor back towards Sammy. He grabbed the chair again and brought it down as hard as he could on his foe's head. A muffled grunt signaled a solid hit and the Woodsman dropped down onto one knee. Sammy repositioned himself and did an underhand swing with the chair. The chair base connected with his face and forced him to lean back, opening up his body.

Charging with the chair in front of him, Sammy yelled and hobbled on both legs for traction and speed, ignoring the pain screaming from his busted leg. The chair legs planted firmly against the Woodsman's chest, Sammy kept pushing as hard as he could. The momentum caused the Woodsman to fall backward onto his tailbone into the hallway. Rage continuing to fuel his actions, Sammy stopped pushing and swung the chair down onto him again, striking his groin. Immediately the Woodsman reflexively curled up into a ball on the floor.

Sammy quickly hopped back to the large desk and ripped out the mouse and cord that were on top. He hopped back to the Woodsman and wrapped the cord around his large neck twice, then pulled hard. Gagging, the Woodsman started flailing his feet, pushing himself back toward the room. He grasped at the cord, trying to free himself. Sammy hopped backward with him, keeping as much pressure on the cord as he could.

Once the Woodsman was halfway into the room, Sammy stopped choking him and went to the far side of the metal cabinet. He pushed it over onto the Woodsman's head, hearing a satisfying crunch from the metal being bent from the force. Sammy climbed on top of the cabinet and began bouncing on it with his good knee, trying to pound it more and more on his head.

After nearly a minute, Sammy finally stopped. He was breathing heavily and was exhausted. Nothing moved underneath the cabinet.

29

    Minutes passed as Sammy slowly calmed down and collected himself. He was sure that he had only managed to knock the Woodsman out, not kill him. But that was only because he didn't have anything lethal enough to do the job, at least not here. But he did in his Jeep.

    He struggled to get back onto his one good leg. It was all he could do to keep from falling over. His loss of blood, lack of food, and dehydration were conspiring to do him in. Slowly he turned towards the small side table, hoping that one of the GPS units had power, since he had lost his in the fall from the church. Something on the wall where the cabinet had been caught his eye, and he looked back at the spot.

    A ladder. Leading up. To an exit door.

    "Holy shit!"

    The ladder was steel and was bolted into the rock wall. Seeing his chance to escape made Sammy nervous and he looked back at the metal cabinet resting on top of the former boxer. He was still out cold, but Sammy wasn't sure for how much longer. He didn't want to leave John down here, but until he took care of their attacker it would be a fruitless rescue.

Returning his attention to the side table, he grabbed the first GPS unit that he laid eyes on. Shoving it into a pocket, he took a chance and picked up the steel water bottle. It was full as he could hear the water slosh around when he shook it. Unscrewing the cap, he took a long drink of cold water. He felt like he was drinking heaven, and quickly polished off the contents. He tossed the bottle and cap onto the table, then started the arduous climb up the steel ladder to what he hoped was freedom.

Climbing the ladder with one bum leg was like trying to climb a rope. He could get leverage with his good leg and push himself up from the rung that he was on. Then he would use his free hands to pull himself up another rung on the ladder, and repeat the process. Fortunately for him, he only needed to do this a few times to be in position to open the door at the top of the ladder. There was a circular handle similar to a hatch door, and it moved easily. He pushed up on the heavy door and it swung back, slamming onto the floor above.

He used the rope climbing technique to raise himself up high enough to poke his head up through the opening and look around. As his eyes got above the floor, he found that he was staring into a wall. He turned to his left and found a wall there as well staring back at him. He turned back and looked to his right and suddenly realized that he knew exactly where he was: the church.

Looking to his right, he was looking from the back left corner of the church toward the front. He had a clear view of the aisle between the left wall and the few pews. The interior of the church was fairly bright, and Sammy wondered just how long he had been down there.

Using the door as leverage, he pulled on it with his left arm and hoisted his upper body over the edge. With both arms he then crawled forward until his legs came up through the hole. He pushed his upper body back onto his legs and got into a kneeling position. From here, he could just see above the pews. His eyes went to the front of the church where the pulpit was, and where his ordeal first started.

Shaking his head to refocus on his situation, he used the closest pew and struggled to his feet. He hopped his way to the back of the church where the door was. He whipped it open and stepped out into the same forest that had once held the promise of a fun weekend. Taking out the GPS unit he had taken from below, he pressed the power button and prayed for it to work.

Nothing happened for a second, then he watched as the screen came to life. A sigh escaped his lips as he saw that the battery was fully charged. Even though it was a model he wasn't familiar with, he quickly grasped the basic key functions. Recalling the general direction that they had taken from camp to get to the church, he used the large digital compass feature and set out towards their camp. Once he had the handgun, he would return to rescue his friend. He only hoped that he would still be alive when he got back.

30

He didn't open his eyes right away. His trainer had always told him that he should give his body a few seconds to recalibrate itself to its present surroundings. Instead, he briefly took stock of his body. His eye still hurt, but not as much as when the chair wheel first hit it. He hoped there was no permanent damage. His head was another matter, as the throbbing began registering in his brain. With each pump of his heart it felt like someone was banging on his head with a sledge hammer.

The rest of his body hurt as well, but not quite as bad. He became aware of a weight on his head, and he finally opened his eyes. Unsure what it was, he used his hands to figure out that it was the metal cabinet that was lying on him. He easily pushed it off his head and it clanged on the floor. The bright light hit his eyes causing the sledge hammers in his head to be joined by a pick ax. He threw his arm over his eyes, easing the pain slightly.

He lay there resting, hoping the pain would subside. And then he suddenly remembered what had happened and why he was on the floor. The little rat bastard somehow got out of his restraints, discovered his secret room with all of the camera feeds, and managed to knock him out even though he had a broken leg and had lost a lot of blood.

He opened his eyes against the harsh light, looking up at the ceiling. Something didn't look quite right to him. He looked around the ceiling, and noticed that the trap door was wide open. The rat bastard had made a second escape. But he wouldn't live to tell the story.

He quickly sat up, which temporarily increased the throbbing in his head. Ignoring the pain, he staggered to his feet and swerved his way down the hall to the room where Sammy had been held. He grabbed down the razor gun from the wall and went back to the camera feed room. He stood the cabinet back up and opened up the doors. He rummaged on a few shelves and finally located what he was after: more razors for the gun. He loaded them into the gun, then took another set of razors and shoved them into his pocket. He pulled out a small box from under the side table and extracted a small air canister, swapping the one on the gun for the fresh bottle.

Pain still emanating from various parts on his body, he pulled himself up the ladder and climbed out into the church. Like a rampaging bull, he burst out through the church doors into the afternoon sunlight. He stopped for a moment, trying to decide which way his prey would have gone.

Familiar. He would go to what's familiar. The Woodsman took off in the direction of their camp.

31

    Hopping and hobbling through a forest was a lot harder than Sammy would have thought, especially since he was trying to do it as quickly as he could. A number of times he had fallen when he lost his balance or when he landed on ground that was softer than anticipated, or if he landed wrong on a tree root. Finally he decided that he needed a crutch of some sort, if only for additional balance. He found a fairly suitable branch that had recently come down in a heavy storm. He stripped off the smaller branches from the main piece in short order and was soon ready to set off again.
    Sammy made good progress, if only because he wasn't falling anymore and having to spend time getting back up. He would occasionally check the compass on the GPS to make sure that he was heading in roughly the right direction. He was confident that if he got fairly close to their camp that he would recognize the terrain and be able to make a beeline back to it quickly.
    As he made his way back to their camp, he kept replaying the images from the monitors in his mind. They haunted him, seeing John covered in blood, not knowing if he was still alive or

not. He shook his head in an effort to wipe away the memories like an Etch-a-Sketch, but they just wouldn't let go.

His arms and good leg were burning in pain from pushing on without a rest. Finally he elected to give himself a few minutes to catch his breath. Leaning up against a large tree, he closed his eyes and tried to focus his thoughts on his current task. Without the visual distraction, he found that he could relax and enjoy the soft sound of the wind blowing through the trees all around him. It was a serene setting, and it helped to calm his mind. He imagined that he was sitting next to a small lake, the bright sun shining down on him, warming him. A light, warm breeze would wash over him. It was his idea of heaven, just sitting out in nature.

Thwack!

Sammy's eyes were open in an instant. He turned his head to the right and saw a round steel blade sticking out of the tree, just inches from his head.

"Oh shit!"

He looked back and saw the Woodsman in the distance. Having missed, the Woodsman started towards him. Sammy grabbed his makeshift crutch and took off as quickly as his mangled body would allow.

32

"Damn! Lucky shit."

The Woodsman watched the blade sink into the bark of the tree just inches from Sammy's head. And now he had given away his position. It was a risky shot since he was so far away, but he was hoping that he could end this sooner rather than later. He started toward Sammy, who took off as he expected.

He was surprised that he had made it this far, being he had the bum leg and the loss of blood. He must have been in really good shape. He would have made a formidable boxer in the ring. But this game was soon going to be over.

The Woodsman worked to close the distance as quickly as he could. His prey was moving pretty good considering his handicap, and the Woodsman had fallen once as he was almost within range to fire another shot. Then Sammy broke out into an open field. It was too large to go around it, so he had decided to go through instead.

The Woodsman got the edge of the clearing and roughly bumped up against a tall pine. He brought the gun up to his shoulder and zeroed in on Sammy's back. Once he had it in sight, he brought the muzzle of the gun up to the back of his head. He made a few adjustments to help compensate for the distance and the slight wind.

"Night, purdy boy."

Pop! Pop!

33

Sammy wasn't sure just how far his Jeep was, but he needed to keep pressing on as fast as he could. That was his immediate need, to make it to the Jeep and the gun. He was using the branch as a sort of stunted high jumper's pole, allowing him to clear a significant distance with each stride. Still, it wasn't as fast as he wanted or could do under normal circumstances.

He could see that a clearing was coming up ahead. He considered going around, but it looked too big and would take too much time. He was better off trying to cross the field as quickly as he could and continuing on. The terrain was becoming a little more familiar to him. He and John had traversed this area a few times going out and coming back that first night, then going back out the next day to continue their geocaching.

As he started out through the field, his paranoia intensified, and it felt like the Woodsman was right behind him. It gave him an extra boost of adrenaline and propelled him forward a little faster. He didn't want to take the chance, even for a moment, to look behind him. It would slow him down and he could stumble and fall, ending his escape. He pushed on, having covered nearly half the distance of the field.

And then he heard the pops in the distance. Instantly he knew what it was, having heard the same sound when he was strapped to the table down below. He hadn't seen anything yet, giving him hope that he had missed again. Then two silver objects shot past him nearly at eye level from his left. Trailing behind them he thought he saw small red droplets.

He couldn't help himself, and he looked down at his left side while he continued to push forward. His leg was fine as was his body and arm. Then he saw fresh blood flowing down the front of his shirt, brighter than the older, darker red splotches from the earlier beating. His skin felt warmer up by his shoulder as well.

Sammy next felt a pain like a snake biting down on his neck. He looked at his shoulder, which was covered in blood. The shock of blood loss hit him, and he stumbled with the branch as his limbs couldn't keep up with his brain's instructions. He fell forward with his right arm out in front and landed hard on his arm and shoulder.

Sammy watched as if watching a television program. The trees rotated from vertical to horizontal, then the camera shook as his body impacted the ground. His body rolled like a log over the ground, arms and legs flailing haphazardly. He finally came to a rest on his side, looking back at the trail of blood and smashed plants.

Everything changed from color to black and white as he laid in the tall grass at the far edge of the field. He watched as the Woodsman walked toward him, gun leaning back against his shoulder. Sammy tried to yell, but nothing came out. His face looked like that of a fish gasping for breath, trying to hold onto life.

He rolled onto his back, thoughts of his friend running through his head. A tear escaped his eye as he realized that he'd failed his friend when he needed him the most. Unable to speak, all he could do was continuously mouth the words I'm sorry.

The Woodsman came to a stand over his prey. A satisfied look covered his face as he looked down, remorse completely absent.

"Gotcha, prick."

34

John raised his head, which felt like it weighed a ton. His neck muscles were sore from being stretched for so long while he was unconscious. The dim light made it hard for him to focus his eyes. Then the Woodsman filled his field of view.

"Your friend put up quite the fight. Can run like a deer, too."

He pulled the slide back on the handgun and released it. He pointed it at John's head.

"Game over."

And he pulled the trigger.

###

ABOUT THE AUTHOR

Darren holds down a normal job by day, and lets his weird side show at night in his writings. He has held a number of different jobs: Financial Analyst, Frozen Food Manager, Pizza Merchandiser, Product Manager, Grocery Bagger, Computer Training Salesperson, Coffee Shop Owner. All along the way, his love of the written word has remained and festered in the far reaches of his mind. Today, he is a budding novelist and short story writer. *"Pins And Dolls"* is his first published short story, and *"Coordinates For Murder"* is his first novel. He lives in the north woods of Wisconsin with his beloved wife and three mischievous felines.

You may reach Darren in a variety of ways:

Website/Blog – darrenkirby.blogspot.com
Email – dlk.writer@gmail.com
Facebook – www.facebook.com/darrenleekirby
Twitter – www.twitter.com/darrenleekirby
LinkedIn – www.linkedin.com/in/darrenkirby

Made in the USA
Monee, IL
10 December 2024